CANCEL SHAWN BOSTON

SAVY LEISER
RK GOLD

Dedicated to all the viewers who watched the creation of this book on livestream for over a year.

Adopt don't shop.

What makes you think I want to be relatable?

Rachel Hollis

Manage your expectations

Gabbie Hanna

I'd rather look good dead and tanned, than pale and alive

Trisha Paytas

You guys asked for it

Dave Hollis

Chapter 1

E veryone suffers for their art, right? Lindsey Drake always tried to believe that, especially on days like these when she was at a mid-sized pop culture convention, splitting a tiny six-foot table with Athena—her best friend and upstairs neighbor—to save on costs.

Today the two were sharing a table in Artist Alley at CreateCon Chicago, and while they'd both made a few sales throughout the morning, they couldn't help but notice the majority of the crowd gathered around a table across from them—all eyes were on one E-Thot McGee.

E-Thot McGee wasn't just a snarky nickname Lindsey came up with to describe the social media influencer. She wasn't *that* full of internalized misogyny. No, E-Thot McGee was her actual stage name. Lindsey couldn't tell if the name was meant to be tongue-in-cheek, or if she was actually a cam-girl or something. Despite being 23 years old and a member of Gen Z, Lindsey wasn't as well immersed in internet culture as her peers.

Lindsey and Athena had been working the Chicago-area convention circuit for the past two years, and both girls could admit they needed to up their game.

Lindsey's side of the table was filled with cute stickers, enamel pins, and patches featuring cartoonish cats dressed up in 80s punk garb. By contrast, Athena's side mostly held cardstock and canvas prints duplicating her oil paintings, which featured Renaissance-style naked women lying in fruit.

Athena's borderline pornographic art, plus Lindsey's natural sales-pitching ability (especially to men; Lindsey was self-aware enough to admit that she wasn't above fake-flirting to make a sale) had kept the money coming in at a steady pace all morning.

Since the convention began at 9 a.m., Lindsey already had three guys—one in Joker cosplay, one in a vintage-style Yu-Gi-Oh! T-shirt, and one wearing E-Thot McGee merch—approach her and ask if she would be their "Big Tiddy Goth GF." Athena looked disgusted each time, but Lindsey casually responded with "Sure, but first you have to buy at least $50 worth of Punk Kitty merch."

That's what Lindsey called "knowing her target audience."

"The customer is always right," she told Athena.

"Your customers are creeps," Athena scoffed.

Athena wasn't wrong. Lindsey currently had a pile of men's phone numbers in the left pocket of her jeans, which she planned to flush down the toilet during her next bathroom break; she also had their cash in her lockbox.

Around noon, Lindsey took stock of her sales. She'd sold around $500 worth of Punk Kitty art and merch, which was short of her $5,000 weekend goal. She *had* to have a good Saturday. Lindsey needed the money to make rent in her shitty studio apartment for the next two months, and to put down a deposit for the biggest convention of the year: New York ArtCon.

Lindsey and Athena had been dreaming of going to New York ArtCon for years. If they wanted to seriously start making a steady, full-time income from their art, they'd have to start going to big conventions like ArtCon, where hundreds of thousands of people browsed artists' tables all weekend long. Unfortunately, ArtCon's smallest tables started at $2,000.

Lindsey looked across the aisle at E-Thot McGee, whose standee boasted her 400,000 subscriber count on YouTube. McGee still had a giant crowd surrounding her table, waiting in line to get their merch signed or to buy new art from her.

McGee's art isn't even that good, Lindsey thought. Not that it was horrible or anything, but Lindsey could tell McGee spent more time growing her internet presence than perfecting her art. She thought that was kind of gross, but she couldn't deny the effect it was having on her sales. Maybe people wanted to buy the artist, not the art.

Lindsey turned to Athena, sitting next to her in their gray folding chairs. "I know social media sucks ass, but hear me out." She could already see Athena beginning to roll her eyes, but she continued anyway. "Do you ever think we could start a YouTube channel or something? We could get more visitors at conventions if we had some kind of fan base, plus we could make additional sales online."

"The whole reason I do conventions rather than selling online is that I don't want my real name out there on the internet," Athena replied sternly. "I don't want people to connect my art and my identity so publicly. It's creepy."

About an hour later, a young woman in a CreateCon Chicago-branded polo stopped by Lindsey and Athena's table to hand them each a thick, stapled packet of papers.

"Here's the early signup forms if you both want to reserve a table for ArtCon this summer," she said.

Lindsey grabbed her pen and immediately began filling out her packet, while Athena glanced at hers more hesitantly. Athena's eyes scanned each page from top to bottom; her fingers held onto the previous page in case she needed to flip back quickly.

"You want to slow down a bit there?" Athena asked. "We don't even know yet if we're going to make enough today to cover the fee."

"Chill," said Lindsey. "I'm not going to actually give them the deposit until after I finish selling. But we *need* to be at ArtCon this year, Athena. Especially if we're not doing the whole online selling thing."

"You know, you could always just start your own online store by yourself," Athena said, continuing to inspect the pages of her own registration packet. "You don't need me to—" Suddenly, Athena stopped talking and her eyes grew wide.

"What is it?" Lindsey asked.

"Oh my God. Elise Shiloh is going to be at ArtCon!"

"Elise Shiloh?"

"She's, like, my idol!" Athena whipped her phone out of her back pocket and pulled up Elise Shiloh's website, *Find Peace with Elise*. She handed her phone to Lindsey, who scrolled through the website for a moment. From the website, Elise Shiloh appeared to be some kind of cross between a new-age hippie and a corporate business coach. Her website was full of platitudes about "investing in yourself" and "unleashing your inner artist," even though no actual art was present on her site.

"Is she even an artist?" Lindsey asked.

Athena shook her head. "No. But I took her Business for Artists course online last year, with a fake name, of course, and it taught me how to get better at sales pitching. I think she's going to be at ArtCon to do some panels or workshops about sales or something."

"Her course sounds like a scam," said Lindsey.

"No, it was so good. It taught me all the sales pitching fundamentals."

"Right, because you're *so* fantastic at sales pitching now." Lindsey rolled her eyes.

Athena playfully slapped her shoulder. "Come on, I'm getting better."

Athena was not getting better at sales pitching. She was shy, reserved, and timid. She never called people over to the table, and when they did come over, she'd often let them browse her work quietly without ever engaging them in conversation.

Lindsey, on the other hand, would yell at passersby, "Come look at my Punk Kitty!" and push out her voluptuous chest.

Half of the guys who passed the table would hurl back, "Can I look at your punk tiddies?"

Athena called that "sexual harassment." Lindsey called it good sales strategy.

Athena continued flipping through her packet, her smile growing bigger by the second.

"What is it?" Lindsey asked. "Elise is offering to suck your cock if you upgrade your table?"

"Shut up," Athena scoffed. "No, she's holding an art contest. She's already accepting submissions now, and she's going to pick five pieces to be featured in her workshop."

Lindsey leaned over to look at the page in Athena's packet. "Oh, that's actually pretty cool," she said.

"Yeah, it could be some great publicity. Maybe this is what I need to get more sales."

"Or we could just try the internet."

"I think I'll try Elise's method before becoming an e-girl, thanks," said Athena.

Elise was kind of an e-girl in her own way, but Lindsey didn't need to say that.

As the day wore on, Lindsey continued to make sales. Athena rifled through her art, trying to choose which piece to submit to Elise for New York ArtCon.

"I guess you're fully sold on ArtCon then, huh?"

"Absolutely!" said Athena, eyeing a plastic-sheathed cardstock print of her oil painting *Grape Nipples*. *Grape Nipples* was one of Athena's best-selling pieces; it featured a naked woman lying on her back in a giant wooden barrel of green grapes, with two purple grapes tastefully covering her nipples. In one hand, she held a glass of white wine and in the other, a glass of red wine. "It's a commentary on capitalism," Athena had told Lindsey. "It looks like soft-core porn," Lindsey had responded. "The mere concept of soft-core porn is a commentary on capitalism in its own way," Athena had retorted.

"Do you think Elise Shiloh will like *Grape Nipples?*" Athena asked Lindsey, who was busy emailing a receipt from her credit card reader app to the customer who'd just left their table.

"I have no idea what Elise Shiloh's sexual preferences are," Lindsey answered.

"No, I mean my painting." Athena held it up.

"Sure," Lindsey shrugged.

By the end of the day, Lindsey hadn't quite reached her $5,000 goal, but she'd come close—$3,500 wasn't terrible for a convention of this size, especially when she had a minor e-celebrity competing with her for crowd attention.

As Lindsey began packing her enamel pins and sew-on patches into her large green duffel bag, Athena positioned

Grape Nipples on the now-empty folding table and began snapping photos of it with her phone.

The same polo-wearing woman came back to their table as Lindsey was folding their tablecloth.

"I'm here to pick up ArtCon registration packets if you have them ready."

"Yes!" Lindsey replied, grabbing the packet out of her bag along with the $1,000 check she'd written for her half of the table. "Here's mine."

The woman took Lindsey's packet, right as Athena whipped out her checkbook. "Here's mine," Athena said. "I'm also entering the Elise Shiloh art contest."

"Did you check the box and write the email address Elise should expect on the appropriate line?" Polo Lady asked.

Athena nodded.

"Great. I'll see both of you at ArtCon in July!"

Lindsey sighed softly. Today had been rough, but ArtCon—the biggest convention she and Athena would have done to date—was coming in just five months.

Lindsey and Athena slung their duffel bags—packed with their merchandise and display items—over their shoulders and trudged out into the frigid Chicago air. Lindsey silently cursed Punxatawny Phil for seeing his shadow again this year. *Couldn't spring come early for once?* she thought.

They each got a seat on the Red Line train outside the convention center, where they finally removed the weight of their duffel bags from their shoulders and placed them on the floor in front of them.

As the train moved above the city, Lindsey remembered something important: if she was to sell thousands of pins, patches, stickers, and prints at ArtCon, she'd better get that inventory ready!

Good thing she'd made $3,500 today. Well, $2,500, since she'd spent $1,000 on her ArtCon table. And if she ordered enough merchandise to sell at ArtCon, she'd have... well, pretty much nothing left.

But that was okay. She was going to sell it all at ArtCon. She'd just have to tell Francisco that she'd be a little late on rent. He'd understand, right?

She pulled up her manufacturer's website on her phone and added more items to her cart than she ever had before. Her finger hovered above the "Place Order" button.

Well, she thought, *it's like Elise Shiloh says: you've got to invest in yourself, babe!*

She submitted the order, waving goodbye to all of today's hard-earned profits.

Chapter 2

F or the first time in years, Rick felt like he could ask someone for their order without them pulling out their phone, pointing to the screen, and laughing at him. The order was nothing special, just a gin and tonic; the double-chinned techie trying to bring back the office lumberjack look paid without another word, his eyes on his phone the entire time.

Most days at the bar, Rick dealt with comments like "Wait, wait, wait, is that you?" usually from some red-nosed college student jabbing their stubby finger at the video of an overweight teen getting thrown to the ground like a sack of dirty laundry by a lanky, grey-haired man. Rick's grandpa, Phil, never spoke of the altercation again. Rick doubted he even knew there was video evidence of it online. As far as Phil was concerned, he won the argument then and there: Rick would not waste his time studying music in school unless he wanted to pay the cost of an apartment and food as well. Phil didn't want him to go into debt for anything he couldn't pay off, so Rick did as he was told. Now he silently grinned through drink orders, a socially acceptable college degree hanging in his bedroom back home. He could barely pay off the frame let alone the piece of paper inside.

His exchanges were easier now. Under the dim light of the comedy club Low Octave, customer interactions were all but scripted and choreographed. Quality and quantities of alcohol, price of the order, exchange bills or plastic for receipt and drinks, and wish the patrons a good night. The routine was as meditative as a handsaw sliding back and forth, the rhythm of its blade drowning out the rest of his thoughts.

He felt his phone vibrate in his pocket leg. His once-baggy jeans were hugging him a little tighter now and he couldn't wedge his fingers into his pocket without drawing attention to himself. It had to be Genie; no one else texted him except census polls and delivery discounts. Before he could covertly wriggle his phone out, a figure appeared in the corner of his eye.

"Delilah's got a flat and no way Billy can go on right now. When'd you cut him off?" his boss, Rufus, asked. He was shorter than Rick, but his enormous nose added at least a foot to his presence—and his demeanor. Even when his boss stood level with his chest, Rick felt the urge to speak up to him. "We need someone on, I can't have dead air right now, people are getting rowdy."

Rowdy wasn't the word Rick would use to describe it. He surveyed the dimly lit round room. Most people were chatting with the rest of their tables or placing their orders. Personally, he hated taking an order when the show started, so he assumed the waiting staff appreciated having a chance to clearly make out the orders.

The building had two parts, a restaurant in the front half where everyone entered, and which doubled as a sports bar (especially when the Bills or Sabres were playing) and the back where the stage rested. The performance room was divided into three sections, and people were ushered in by their ticket letters 20 minutes before the show started; A tickets seated closest to the stage or in the comfortable booths in the back corners, B tickets taking up most of the middle tables, and C in the wings. Only those closest to the stage were making noise. Rick usually stayed in the restaurant area, behind the bar where he could hide from the crowds.

"I need you." Rufus jabbed a finger into Rick's solar plexus so firmly he had to grit his teeth to stop an accidental groan from exiting his mouth.

"I'm not a comedian," Rick replied as he handed a beer to the blonde beside his boss. She snuck under his armpit to get it, shooting him a side-eye as he left.

"I'm not a moron, Dick," Rufus shot back, preferring the phallic nickname—or as he called them, dicknames—anyone with the misfortune of being named Richard was familiar with. "But you got the house drums in the back. I think Beth could hop on the guitar. You two probably know at least one cover."

"You want us to hopefully know one song we can repeat until Billy sobers up?" Rick tried not to roll his eyes.

"Come on, they need something. If they just wanted each other's company, they would've stayed home trying to fingerbang to a sitcom on Netflix."

"That's way too specific," Rick chuckled as a couple approached the bar.

"I'll ask Beth," Rufus slapped the counter twice and pointed a sausage-shaped forefinger at Rick as he walked away.

.   .   .

When food began to come out and still no performers had graced the stage, the casual conversations at the tables turned into a performance of "Spartacus", only everyone was renamed "Refund." Rufus returned shaking his head.

"Beth knows the piano, not the guitar." He mimed the keys then shrugged, as if it was a simple mistake to confuse the two instruments. "You're on." He clapped his hands.

"Me? Alone without a guitarist? What do you want me to do for melody, hmm?"

"People don't care what they're hearing. They just wanna hear something." As he spoke, cheers came from the front of the restaurant. Only a few tables close to the restaurant area managed to sneak back over and grab a bar stool; the restaurant was packed for the Sabres-Flyers game. As the cheers erupted, the quiet back room turned to the front doors. Rick could hear them contemplating their decision to come out, like they'd accidentally chosen the loser table in the cafeteria all over again and were longing to sit in the cool section.

"Come on kid, just get up there and play something."

Rick looked back to the stage. No one was coming up to order any more drinks. The closest table had four people uniformly folding their arms, and at the table beside them was an overweight man sleeping with his mouth wide open. A man at the front slapped the empty stage, shouting "Come on already!"

"I *need* you." Rufus's tone softened and he pressed his hands together. His fingers weren't perfectly steepled, giving the impression he'd either never prayed before or had lost practice. "You're always back there playing behind the curtains between acts. I'm just asking you to do it in front of the curtain."

Rick's heart raced in his chest. He looked down into Rufus' eyes for the first time that night. Of course, he knew what his boss was requesting, and that was exactly why he couldn't bring himself to do it. He was familiar with spotlights, having been in several since he was seventeen. Behind the curtains he could drop a stick or miss a step and the audience would forget the sound the second the next performer grabbed the microphone. He could even handle a nod to the anonymous man behind the curtains for keeping tempo that night. But coming out to the front of the stage in full view of the light, where everyone could see him while their faces were masked in shadows? No, he couldn't return to that.

"I can't," he replied, but the words came out more like a cough. The kind of cough that's forced out when your back hits the sidewalk and the sun is blocked out by the hovering figure of your 70-year-old recently divorced grandfather.

"Whatever, kid." Rufus turned away without any snide remarks or name-calling. Instead, he made his way to the stage and grabbed the microphone, his words blurred out by a ringing in Rick's ears. They waited another thirty minutes for Delilah to get there, and Billy in his still-inebriated state crashed on stage, nearly taking down the curtains in the process.

Rick could hear patrons' mumblings about the shitty night and the "I'm not coming back here anytime soon" whispers as the crowd ushered themselves out. The bar was especially quiet since the Sabres lost, and the celebratory drinks turned into DUI roulette.

Rick decided not to stick behind after their shift to have drinks with the rest of the staff, though none of them spoke to him differently. Beth gave him a hug and a pat on the head, and Drew wished him well before Rick headed out. Only Rufus couldn't look his way, but the rough evening wasn't Rick's fault. He wasn't paid to entertain the crowd; his boss put him in an uncomfortable position. Why should he be required to go outside his comfort zone? Not to mention, any time away from the bar was time not earning tips. Would Rufus reimburse him for that missed opportunity?

His hands in fists, he stomped with a little extra *oomph* as he left the bar and was ready to rage quit by the time he made it to the bus stop. He bounced up and down in place, looking back and forth for his bus, ready to get out of the cold and get home. Each second, he didn't see the head-lights raised his pulse a little more and made his jaw clench a little tighter.

Rick and his grandpa lived in a red brick apartment just off Allen Street. The sidewalk had a rainbow flag painted along its street-side edge, and the music from the bars carried through down the street. His landlord, Sven, was in the foyer putting away a mop and placing a yellow wet floor sign outside the elevators as Rick walked in.

Sven's silver hair was brushed back, and his sleeveless shirt hugged his toned frame. He wasn't much younger than Rick's grandpa, and it felt like his body existed solely to torment Rick's clearly broken metabolism. "Was hoping to have a word with you," he sounded like a concerned school principal.

"About the rent? Look, I know my grandpa can get a little Houdini when you start talking about money. Have you been able to find him?" Rick replied.

"Tried calling, knocking, even emailing in case he had trouble with his phone again." Sven flicked an open hand across his throat. "Nothing."

"How much do we owe?"

"Don't worry about it, kid, that's for me and him to work out. Downstairs is empty if you're wondering. I'm not getting to it 'til tomorrow morning." Sven smirked and exited through the side door to the spiral stairs that went directly to the top floor. Rick needed to blow off some steam, and nothing cleared his mind faster than a four-on-the-floor beat with some heavy cymbals. But he needed to hear from someone first. An angry vent session would douse his feelings like alcohol on an open cut.

Genie answered his FaceTime call on the first ring, leaving her camera turned off. She left Rick to talk to a half-erased purple dragon. "Hey! I was just having a dream that you'd go a day without needing me," she said.

"Very funny. Look, I need some advice."

"Yeah, no shit. You always need advice."

Rick rolled his eyes, forgetting he always had his camera on when they spoke, and was met with a blast of laughter. "You're so sassy, Ricky," Genie added with a sympathetic chuckle that always shifted the laughter from at him to with him.

He recounted the story of work, with a few minor embellishments. "So, Rufus jabbed his finger into my chest and bent forward so I was practically doing the limbo." And "I'm pretty sure he threatened to fire me if I didn't go on, and how unfair is that? Where is performing in my job description?"

Genie cut in after every tidbit, never letting Rick gain too much momentum. "Did he really?" and "I thought he was barely five feet; how was he towering over you?"

Still, they both laughed by the end of the last detour. "So, what do you think?"

"About what, your boss? Rufus has been kind of a dick since you started working there, but he's never been irredeemably dickish."

"You know what a club is like when the crowd is mad? They were just looking for someone to boo. You really want me to be the sacrifice? They would've pinned the whole night on me. I'd probably be the scapegoat for the Sabres loss, too, if I'd gone onstage."

"But you would've been paid to play."

"I'm already paid to play; what do you think my job is there?" Rick sat on the top step to the basement and closed the door. He tapped his hand on his thigh as if counting himself in on a song.

"Get drunk?" Genie suggested, and Rick stifled a grin. "I know you play in between jokes there, but come on, don't you want to perform? Isn't that why you started in the first place?"

"If I wanted to be seen, I wouldn't have picked the instrument that puts me in the very back of the stage."

"Sounds like you choked, to me."

"Choked? How did I choke? Cause I didn't want to make a fool of myself in front of a crowd of angry people?"

"Would they have been angry if you played?"

"I don't know. I'd have to tell you after recovering from a bottle being thrown at my head."

"Now I know you're exaggerating; at worst, they'd boo you."

"Maybe I've had enough of that in my life, thank you." Rick turned his camera off and set the phone down next to him on the step.

"Don't get all moody," Genie said.

"You just don't understand," Rick said.

Genie snorted. "I've been friends with you for how many years? You always say the same thing, like you're permanently branded—"

"I'm just now getting my life back. Finally," Rick cut in.

"Sounds like you're finally getting your excuses back, is all."

"Suck a dick."

"I just think if you go your whole life trying to be invisible you might get exactly what you want."

"I don't see the problem."

"Maybe *that's* the problem, and by the time you realize it, it'll be too late."

Rick gritted his teeth. "I think I gotta help my grandpa with the heat. I'll talk to you later." He hung up and pocketed his phone. She had no idea what it was like to go through what he had. And to suggest that just being friends with him gave her an understanding was just... *nope*. He shook his head and walked down to his drums. The second he closed the door, his jaw loosened and all the muscles in his back relaxed. In this space, he didn't have a job or a family. He didn't have a degree or a hometown. All he had was a 1-2-3-4, 1-2-3-4, the numbers repeated in his head as he hit the kick drum.

Chapter 3

The weekend after a mid-sized convention, Lindsey always liked to decompress. She spent the following Saturday night in her cramped Chicago studio apartment, sitting naked at her small IKEA desk, drawing some new Punk Kitty designs.

Lindsey propped her left foot up on her desk, swiveling herself around slightly in her desk chair, while she held her stylus in her right hand. Her drawing tablet was connected to her outdated MacBook laptop, and she had Photoshop open with a new Punk Kitty file.

To drown out the world around her, Lindsey wore giant noise-canceling headphones and had a playlist of background music on YouTube. She was listening to a new musician she'd found recently named Shawn Boston. He'd apparently gotten pretty big a few years ago making music videos and posting them on YouTube, and now he had over 50 million subscribers. His music was decent, too. Nothing about it was amazing or innovative or groundbreaking, but it provided some nice chill background sounds while Lindsey worked on her art.

Shawn's music videos were tagged as "indie" in the description box. They mostly featured Shawn playing his acoustic guitar and singing softly, usually vague songs about love or other things.

Lindsey preferred when songs about love kept it vague. She hadn't had any kind of love life since she broke up with Chad the Cheater at the end of college. At the time, she had been living in an apartment with Chad and her older brother, Tony—who happened to be Chad's best friend. Athena had warned her against dating her brother's best friend, but Athena was an only child, so what did she know? But as it turned out, Athena was right, and when Lindsey found out Chad had been banging half the girls who came into the coffee shop where he worked, she immediately dumped his ass. She assumed that Tony would kick Chad out of their apartment, considering that Lindsey was his sister and blood is supposed to be thicker than water. Instead, he sided with his friend, believing all Chad's lies that Lindsey had "made him cheat" by always declining sex. Lindsey and Tony hadn't spoken for nearly two years since she moved into the studio apartment on the floor below Athena.

Lindsey worked on shading the side of a new lime green version of Punk Kitty. She highlighted some bright streaks in his fur, matching where his solid black eyes glistened.

The second Shawn Boston's third vague love song ended; Lindsey heard a loud SLAM erupt from her door. She slid her headphones down around her neck and swiveled around in her chair, facing the door.

SMACK. SLAM. THUNK.

Lindsey froze. Was someone breaking in? She rushed over to her front door and looked through the peephole. A half-bald, middle-aged Italian man stood close, with one hand on his hip and the other raised near the door, ready to pummel it again. Her landlord, Francisco. Of course.

"I'm coming!" she yelled, as Francisco banged the door hard enough to shake the doorknob loose. When the doorknob rattled, she heard Francisco yell, "Oh, God damn it, Lindsey!" from the other side of the door.

Lindsey quickly grabbed a throw blanket off the foot of her bed and wrapped it around her naked body. She swung the door open, pulling the doorknob all the way off in the process.

"Finally, you answer!" Francisco yelled. "How hard do I have to bang the door? How many times are you going to make me fix this doorknob for you?"

Francisco was always the reason the doorknob even needed to be fixed, but Lindsey wasn't going to tell him that. Not when his face resembled a tomato, both in shape and color.

"Sorry," she mumbled.

"Where are your clothes? You got a revolving door of men in here, or what?"

"No, I just wasn't dressed."

"Good. Be careful with all the kissing. Some of my family back in Italy, they are dealing with this new coronavirus."

"What?" Lindsey asked.

"A new virus. It's going everywhere. Just be careful who you get too close to! In Italy, it's so bad they have to force people to stay in their houses. Everybody's work is shut down. They all have to work online. I am praying to Jesus it doesn't get that bad here!" He crossed his chest and kissed his silver cross. It was the only accessory that stood out on him, and she never saw him without it.

Lindsey decided that tonight she'd say a prayer for the same thing, even though she wasn't religious. She definitely couldn't work online if that happened; especially not when she'd just put down such a huge deposit for ArtCon.

"What do you need, Francisco?" she asked.

"Your boxes are clogging up the whole hallway downstairs!" he yelled.

"My boxes?"

"Yes! Twenty-eight boxes from some company called CuteStuff Manufacturing! Why do you order so much?"

My new merchandise, Lindsey thought. She hadn't expected it to come so quickly. In the past, she'd have to wait up to three or four months to get her stuff. They must not have had many other orders to get through this time. "Sorry, it's for work."

Francisco rolled his eyes. "Well, put some clothes on and come down to get your boxes! Nobody else's deliveries can fit in the front!" Francisco turned on his heel and stormed down the hallway. "And you are paying to fix that doorknob!" he shouted back.

Once Francisco was gone and the door was locked, Lindsey threw her blanket back onto the couch and darted over to her bed to find some clothes. She flopped stomach-first down onto the bed, with her head hanging over the side, as she searched for clothes along her floor and underneath the bed. Lindsey couldn't remember the last time she'd done laundry. Probably sometime within the last two weeks, right? Or else she'd be out of underwear by now. Well, maybe not. Lindsey spent most of her time at home completely naked with the heat cranked all the way up— another reason Francisco hated her. Her portion of the utility bill barely covered her personal consumption of the building's heat.

"Why don't you just wear a sweater?" Francisco had angrily asked Lindsey back in December. The building's electric bill that month showed that Lindsey's 500-square-foot studio apartment had used over $400 of electricity.

"I can't fit boobs this big into a sweater," she'd replied, knowing that Francisco would have no way to respond to that without making it weird.

Now, Lindsey was searching her floor for a bra to hold up said giant boobs. A petite woman at 5'2", managing J-cup boobs was no easy feat. But Lindsey could start saving up for breast reduction in the distant future, long after she'd finished paying off her college debt and her convention fees and everything else. In the meantime, she'd just use them to her advantage, no matter how gross Athena thought that was.

Lindsey squeezed into an ugly beige-colored bra she found swimming in a pile of sweatpants underneath the bed. Then she put on Chad's old sweatshirt that she'd stolen after they broke up. If she was going to be left without an apartment, at least she could get a free XXL sweatshirt out of it.

She shimmied into a pair of pajama pants and slid on some old beat-up knockoff Ugg boots she'd bought from a shady re-seller outside of a McDonald's. Then, she headed toward the elevator.

When she reached the lobby, Lindsey finally understood why Francisco was so mad: there were A LOT of boxes, and they were huge.

Lindsey's apartment building had 25 floors, a giant lobby with a few armchairs and a Keurig machine, and a small mailroom off to the left of the lobby, right next to the elevators. Lindsey's boxes covered the entire floor area of the mailroom section; even stacked 3 boxes high, they were starting to spill out into the lobby.

Well, now Lindsey had to find somewhere to put these. They certainly weren't going to fit in her tiny apartment, not if she still expected to have a bed to sleep on. Plus, how was she even going to get them into the elevator? These MIGHT be able to make it up in two or three trips if she used the FREIGHT elevator, but Lindsey was pretty sure Francisco wasn't going to trust her with a freight elevator key. She sighed, hands on her hips, staring at the boxes.

"Staring at the boxes all day is not going to move them out of my lobby, Miss Drake!" Francisco yelled.

"Just give me a minute," Lindsey said, rubbing her forehead. "I'll figure out where to move them, okay?"

"You have two hours, or else they go in the dumpster out back!" Francisco yelled.

No, not the dumpster—Lindsey could NOT lose this much inventory, not after she'd spent almost all of last weekend's profits on it. That left one option: her parents.

Thomas and Eleanor Drake had an unfinished basement at their house on the other side of the city, which basically served as their own personal storage unit. It rarely leaked, and the moisture down there was fairly under control, so theoretically they *could* store everything. But Lindsey tried to limit the number of times she talked to her parents.

Her parents weren't bad people or anything. Lindsey had watched enough Dr. Phil to know how much worse she could've had it. But her parents weren't really what anyone would call "supportive." They always thought Lindsey's art was a phase she was going to grow out of one day; when she told them, she had decided to pursue selling art at conventions as her full-time job, they looked like they were going to have a heart attack. Tony was always the practical one in their eyes. Tony finished a four-year bachelor's degree, which he covered fully through business fraternity scholarships, and then got a job in consulting for some big corporation. The kind of job with *benefits*.

Lindsey could barely get a friend with benefits, let alone a *job* with them.

Lindsey, on the other hand, had taken two years off after high school, then got an associate's degree in graphic design, paid all out of pocket. Well, out of the bank's pockets, as Lindsey still owed almost four grand in loans. Her parents tried not to show their disappointment whenever the family met up for holidays or birthdays, but they always had some not-so-subtle comment like, "So, are you doing okay? With, ya know, money?"

From what Lindsey had seen on TV, parents who normally asked if their kids were doing okay with "you know, money" usually offered them some money if they said "no." However, Lindsey's parents didn't actually have a ton of money to spare, so when Lindsey said, "No, I'm barely making rent," they would instead offer her tons of suggestions of "real jobs" she could get.

When Lindsey started making decent money selling art at conventions and craft fairs, her parents started to soften up to the idea a little, but their occasional side comments made it clear that they would have much more faith in her if she'd taken a path like Tony's.

Still, what choice did she have? They were the only people she knew with a basement. Lindsey fished her cell phone out of the front pocket of Chad's old, oversized sweatshirt and called her parents from the lobby.

"Hello?" her mom answered.

"Hey, Mom, it's Lindsey."

"Oh, Lindsey! I was just going to call you."

"You were?"

"Yes! Lindsey, have you heard about this new virus?"

"Francisco mentioned that his family in Italy—"

"Who's Francisco? A new guy?" Lindsey couldn't tell if her mom's voice was hopeful or disappointed.

"No, he's my landlord."

"Oh, that's right. His family has the virus?"

"No, but parts of his family's town in Italy have been shut down—"

"Yes, that's what's happening! I'm worried that the virus is going to come to Chicago. I heard from Aunt Susan that Washington state is already shutting down! She's had to do all her work on one of those video programs online! And her husband might get laid off."

"I'm sorry to hear that," Lindsey said. This was getting scary. Lindsey had no idea what she'd do if the virus shut down everything around her—she still had about twelve mid-sized conventions to go before ArtCon in July. And... what if the virus was still going on when ArtCon was supposed to happen?

Lindsey couldn't let herself think about those things right now; not when there was an entire mailroom full of her boxes that she was going to lose if she didn't move them out in 2 hours. "So, um, the reason I called—"

"You don't need money, do you?"

"No, Mom. I've never asked you for money."

"You've implied that you need it." Lindsey did need money, but she wasn't about to ask for it.

"That's not what I'm calling about."

"Okay, then. If not money, what do you need? A favor?"

"Just a small one," said Lindsey. "See, I just ordered all my inventory for ArtCon—"

"What is ArtCon? It sounds like 'con artist.' Are you sure it's not a scam?"

Lindsey rolled her eyes, grateful that her mom couldn't see her facial expression over the phone. "ArtCon is the biggest art convention in New York. I'm going to it this July. I told you that last time we talked."

"You know I can't keep all these art events straight. There are so many of them."

"Right, because it's my job."

"If it was your job, then why do you need money?"

Lindsey felt her muscles tensing up. She took a deep breath and let it out slowly, as quietly as possible, so her mom couldn't hear how frustrated she was getting. "Again, Mom, I'm not asking for money. I'm asking for a small favor. So, all my boxes of merchandise arrived today, and it was earlier than I expected. I was wondering if I could store it in your basement."

"Lindsey, you know we don't have that much room in our basement."

"You mostly use it for storage anyway, though."

"Dad is trying to set up a home gym in there."

"Dad doesn't even work out."

"He bought a yoga mat and some free weights. He's going to get back in shape."

Dad was never in shape in the first place, Lindsey thought, but at least she had the sense not to say that out loud. "So, you can't store a few boxes for me?"

"I don't think we'll be able to do that, no. Lindsey, if you think this art thing is your full-time job, then you're going to need to treat it like one. Full-time jobs don't require favors from your parents."

"So, what should I do then?"

"You could rent a storage unit."

An hour later, Lindsey had borrowed Athena's giant hand cart and had stacked about half of her boxes on top of it. After searching around on her phone, Lindsey found that there was a storage facility about three blocks away from her apartment called PackDaddy. She had never considered storing her things there in the past because she'd always just kind of assumed PackDaddy was a gay

26

bar. But as it turns out it was a storage rental facility, and she could pay them a couple hundred dollars to store most of her boxes there until July. After putting three of the boxes in her apartment to use for next week's indoor art festival, she loaded a bunch of the others on Athena's cart, ready to walk three blocks in the below-zero February weather of Chicago.

Bundled in her knit beanie, fingerless gloves, and puffy zip-up coat (Lindsey couldn't do button-down coats due to the boob issue), Lindsey stood at the entrance of the apartment, confirming her storage reservation.

Well, there went the rest of her savings. ArtCon had *better* be good this year.

Chapter 4

His phone vibrating on his face made a better alarm clock than the default beep he never bothered to change. Rolling over in bed and seeing the text from Genie, Rick wondered if his friend ever slept.

"What do you want?" he texted and made his way around his room, attempting to kick socks and underwear on the floor into the hamper, but mostly hitting the wall and his desk lamp. He opened his laptop. The old hinge yawned every time he opened its mouth and a rainbow wheel greeted him longer than most of his first dates. He knew the chance of affording a new laptop was a long shot, but he hoped those long nights at Low Octave would land him enough for a new one, plus a drum pad so he could actually make some money with music online without having to perform live.

"You know I always love your hellos," read Genie's text. "Look, I was just thinking about our conversation yesterday."

Here it came: the apology. He knew he could count on it whenever she pushed him to the point of a speedy exit.

He waited expectantly, his eyes darting back and forth from the three dots on his phone screen to his computer, which finally finished loading. He pulled up two tabs: an Indeed search for job openings where he could put his degree to use, and a Google search for affordable replacement models for his computer.

"And I really think you're missing out when you're handed these opportunities," said Genie's text.

"That's a funny way of saying you're sorry."

"Sorry for what? You do need to grow a pair."

Rick rolled his eyes. He was tempted to toss his phone out the window, but it would be another thing to replace, so he aimed at his bed instead. The device crashed into his pillow. He paced through the maze of t-shirts, athletic shorts, and other garments on the floor, picking a few socks up as he went and tossing them into the hamper before returning to his phone.

"You know you're talented, right? You spend almost all your free time in the basement practicing and the rest of the time talking to me. Don't forget I've heard you! I know what you can do."

Rick didn't usually record himself, but he had sent some videos to Genie in the past, and more than once he'd FaceTimed her as he played along to some of her favorite music. "That's different. Rufus literally wanted me on stage with my dick in my hand."

"What's the problem? You have a HUGE dick!" Genie shot back.

Rick turned back to his computer and saw no responses to his applications. Not even an interview request. He clenched his jaw.

The only reason he even had this stupid business degree was his grandpa. "You're never gonna get a job studying that music nonsense. It's just a hobby and I'm not saying you gotta quit, just make sure you keep your priorities straight," his grandpa lectured him five years ago when he was about to start college. And when Rick insisted his top priorities included music, his grandpa had doubled down. "Well then you'll have to start making money from it soon, cause I won't let you live here rent free if you aren't learning how to take care of yourself."

Rick still went into debt, but his grandpa assured him all through his studies that it would pay for itself as long as he stayed on the right course. Either Rick had grossly misjudged the right course, or his grandpa was a fucking liar.

When he picked up his phone, he saw three messages from Genie:

"You there?"

"Jesus dude it was a joke."

"You're way too sensitive today."

Rick laid back on his bed, ignoring the crinkling sound of an empty chip bag under his pillow. He texted back: "I'm just tired of feeling trapped in a life I didn't sign up for. The moment I start feeling like I have control over it, someone else tries to push me."

"It's life, dude. The more you think you control, the less you do."

"Thanks, fortune cookie."

"Oh, shut up. You know I'm right :P."

Rick didn't know that. Accepting that Genie was right meant all the hard work he put in the previous years meant nothing.

He didn't ask to be thrown into the spotlight when his grandpa sucker-punched him into fame. He had to read through all those comments and walk away from all social media because pictures of him were used to end arguments and taunt people for things as meaningless as video games.

Memes of his grandpa flipping him to the ground brought even the most polarizing arguments to a momentary inter-mission. And Genie wanted him to believe all that was the will of the universe. His choice to remove himself from online discourse wasn't even a choice, but a predetermined sequence he had to experience.

He couldn't lay in bed anymore. Kicking himself up, he left the room, momentarily freezing to catch the hamper his hip nearly knocked over. The pounding in his head grew louder and he needed to release it. He needed to get to his drums. He made his way to the basement and heard voices carrying up the stairs. He crept down and saw Sven's office door was open.

"I forgave you the first month, but I'm starting to think you're fucking with me," Sven said, sounding as casual as a friend asking to borrow a beach chair.

Rick snuck to the side room with his drums and closed the door most of the way. Inside, the room was insulated with egg cartons and foam to keep the sound of his playing from reverberating through the building. When he'd first started playing drums in the basement, the second-floor apartment began shouting about not paying rent to live at a disco. But rather than kick Rick out, Sven had offered to give him a ride to get sound-proofing materials since he needed to get new building supplies anyway.

"I know, such a waste. We could be fucking *each other*," someone replied. Wait, not just *someone*—he knew that voice. It was his grandpa. Rick dropped his drumsticks. He held his breath and scrambled to pick them up. Poking his head out the door, his heart raced as he expected to see the two men looking right at him.

Not only did they not notice, but through the crack in the door, Rick saw the two men staring deep into each other's eyes. His throat tightened and he flipped the door shut. It didn't help. The image of his grandpa leaning forward and Sven meeting his gaze was branded on the inside of his eyelids. Closing his eyes only made the image clearer in his head; he needed to drown it out.

When he sat at the drums, the pounding in his head was replaced by a cyclone. He saw Rufus squeezing his hands together begging him to take the stage as the patrons chanted "Refund!" from their seats. Then, he remembered Sven in the front hall, looking for his grandpa; they had to pay rent—but the way they looked at each other now... *No!* Rick slammed his sticks against the snare drum, and they bounced out of his hands.

Again, his life was falling into someone else's hands. He'd lost his major, his future, and now he could lose his home, all because he let other people make his decisions for him.

Recovering his sticks, he pushed back the images, each strike of the drumhead drowning out the memories. Ever since that video of his fight with Grandpa had gone viral, Rick had spent months at a time locked in this basement room, drumming each comment and thread making fun of him out of his head until all he heard was the music. Even as he sweat and his breath picked up, he felt the anger fade through the vibrations in the air. It was like the frequencies perfectly aligned with him and he sank back into reality, no longer caught up in a disruptive force.

By the time he finished, he felt new. He wiped the sweat off his face with the bottom hem of his baggy t-shirt and started back upstairs. If his grandpa needed more help with rent, he knew what he had to do; he had to offer to start performing at work more. It wouldn't be much, but it could add up.

When he made it back to the apartment, he was relieved to see his grandpa digging around in the refrigerator. He pulled out eggs and cheese and started preparing lunch for himself. Rick didn't bother to ask if he'd toss in a couple extra, knowing the response would be along the lines of, "Wait til I'm done and do it yourself."

"Did you hear about Sven's grandson? They're worried about a lockdown. He's been working out of his apartment for almost a week," Grandpa said from in front of the stove.

"That's intense," Rick replied, sitting down in a kitchen chair. He wondered what he would do if he were trapped in the apartment for a week, assuming Sven didn't throw them out on their asses. There was no way he and his grandfather could last in the apartment together. Rick would probably spend the entire time in the basement.

"Where're you coming back from, anyway? You're looking sweaty." His grandpa cracked two eggs in the frying pan.

"Just jamming," Rick tapped the counter. The galley through the kitchen barely fit them both, and he brushed against his grandpa's back as he reached across to grab a sports drink out of the fridge. The counter was clean of all food and the cutting board was freshly scrubbed. All the knives, spatulas, and cooking utensils were organized on a rack next to the sink which still had bubbles on it from when his grandpa cleaned it.

"You should be at your computer looking for jobs so you can get out of that club."

"I've applied to over fifty jobs—"

"So not even one a week."

Rick bit back a response. He wasn't ready to throw a jab with what he heard about the rent when he was downstairs. "I get paid this week. Wouldn't make sense to quit now and miss out on two more shifts."

"Only two," his grandpa snorted. "Do you have any

idea how much I was working when I was your age? I swear, you just want everything to come easy, don't you? Spending all day playing around with that… that hobby of yours and being happy about two extra shifts."

"Is something bugging you?" Rick asked, hoping he wouldn't have to pressure his grandpa too much, especially after seeing the way he and Sven were looking at each other. He didn't need to relive that brief moment of silence.

To his surprise, his grandpa cracked open a couple more eggs and slid the plate of two sunny-side up eggs and buttered toast across the counter for Rick to grab. Rick kept his eyes on his grandpa as he re-entered the kitchen, sure he would stop him at any moment and question why Rick was trying to steal his lunch, but to Rick's surprise, Grandpa even handed him a fork before turning his attention back to the stove.

"I guess I've been a little stressed lately," his grandpa sighed. Rick took his first bite, not minding that his grandpa went light on the butter.

"About the rent?" his voice squeaked as he doubted if he should ask the question all the way up to the point of speaking it. As soon as the words fully left his mouth, he tightened up. His grandpa silently began mixing the eggs a little faster.

"What *about* the rent?" he finally asked as he poured the scrambled yolks into the frying pan. "Were you listening down in the basement?"

"A bit, but Sven said he was looking for you yesterday, so it's not like I had no idea," Rick replied. There was no reason for his grandpa to push him back on his heels. He did nothing wrong by hearing their conversation; it was his apartment too, and the only reason he wasn't paying half the rent was his grandpa's insistence that he save what he would pay until he could properly invest.

"If you were listening, then you'd know I have everything under control."

Under control? Rick wondered. It didn't sound like he had anything under control. All he knew was his grandpa made a sex joke and—"It wasn't a joke," he mumbled to himself.

"Excuse me?"

"Are you fucking Sven for rent?"

"Where the fuck did that come from?" His grandpa smacked the spatula against the counter and Rick shuttered. Last time his grandpa sounded this angry, it ended up with 90 million views.

"I've been saving like you asked, but if you need money, let me help," Rick insisted. But his grandpa shook his head. "You wanna help, stop kicking around in the basement and get a job, a real job, not one that's pouring drinks, so people think a shitty routine is funny."

"No one is hiring," Rick's voice rose. They had this talk every week. Like his grandpa couldn't equate the simple math of one degree doesn't always equal one job. In fact, it mostly just meant one hell of a huge debt.

"Then you go to them, and you don't leave until you get the job!"

"Or if I'd just studied music, I'd be working somewhere that needed me! Or freelancing or something. But no, you had to force me to—"

"Force you? I didn't force you not to study music. You were just too afraid to head out on your own."

Rick clenched his jaw. They had been down this road many times before, his grandpa always claiming he had every right to study whatever he wanted as long as he respected his grandfather's right to not support him with rent. "That's not the point."

"Sure, it is," his grandpa insisted. "You're pissed you made the wrong decision and you're looking for someone to blame instead of fixing it." He sucked the excess butter off his thumb and bit into his toast.

"You're such an asshole. I was hoping to talk about helping you with rent if you needed it so you wouldn't impress yourself with Sven." Rick started for the door. He needed to get away.

"And you know what an insult that is to me," Grandpa practically growled back. A vein in his neck bulged.

Rick knew all too well how his grandpa got whenever money was brought up. Grandpa had promised Rick's parents he'd look after him if anything ever happened to them. They dropped him off at his grandparents' house when they lived in Snyder, where neighbors raised their kids to be congressmen, and took off on a relief mission. He didn't know how long they were supposed to be gone for, more interested in how many goldfish he could fit in his pocket during snack time than anything else, but when his birthday came, then Christmas and New Years and summer vacation, all without a word from them, his grandparents' promises that everything was fine began to sound hollow.

"Maybe if you stopped that stupid hobby and focused on something real, you'd be able to get your life in order and move out," his grandpa added as Rick reached the front door.

"No wonder grandma left you for that biker chick!" he shouted back.

"Try saying that to my face if you want a repeat of last time," Grandpa challenged before Rick could even slam the door.

No matter how hard he played, he couldn't drown out the argument. "If you want a repeat of last time." He couldn't shake that remark. It was one memory he wished he could erase forever, but even if he could, it would only be a matter of time until someone brought it up at work again.

Despite the five years that had passed, the memory was still fresh in his mind. Rick was looking over his class schedule. It was the first time he had sat down in the past week. He was still wearing his work shirt with Club Low Octave's golden logo on it. Between his new job, preparing for some big internet comedian's show that weekend, and the move, he hadn't had a moment to himself. He and his grandpa were moving all the furniture they could carry on their own out of the rented U-Haul. He always loved Allentown, and his friends with fake IDs frequented the bars along Allen Street. There was plenty of live music too, and maybe, he thought with a smile, one day he could play at the bars too.

His grandpa assumed he was signing up for business classes; Rick had promised to give it a try, maybe he would even double major in it, but getting accepted into the music department was where he felt he belonged.

"Oh, good, you found time to sit down. That must mean we're done," his grandpa said as he lined up an end table next to the couch. "Whatcha got there anyway?" he reached for the paper, but Rick quickly pulled it away and started out of the apartment. "What else do you need me to get?"

"I need your help with the desk, but hold on a second,

is that your class schedule?" he pointed to the sheet as they both reached the front door. Rick pocketed the paper and climbed into the back of the truck.

"Yeah, just signed up for my first classes, a lot of 101 stuff," he shrugged but his grandpa maintained a skeptical stare. His eyes lingered on Rick's pocket even as his grandson tried to lift the desk completely on his own, lifting with his back and straining his muscles. Rick's breath came out in trumpet-like spurts and his face went red. He collected himself and tried to lift the desk again, only getting it an inch off the ground on his own before putting it back down to catch his breath.

"I think I'd like to see it," his grandpa stated emphatically.

"Why?" Rick replied, knowing any refusal would only inspire more of his grandfather's curiosity. What if he called the school and found out? Could he even do that? And would he even be mad if Rick was taking music? It wasn't like he was refusing to take anything else. He still had general ed credits to take, and he could probably fit in a finance class.

Knowing he had been quiet for way too long and grasping for anything to say before his grandpa could ask once again, Rick added, "Uh, the Sabres—" but it was too late. His grandpa hopped into the truck and reached into Rick's pocket. Rick tried his best to swat Grandpa's hands away, but his grip made Rick feel like he was made of cotton candy. He expected the indentations to be permanent by the time his grandpa pulled away.

Trying his best to stand tall, Rick's heart raced. He doubted he could get a single word out without coughing to the beat of his pulse.

It didn't take long for his grandpa to finish skimming the page, but the silence between them stretched out time.

Each inhale felt like it lasted over a minute, and when they finally locked eyes again, the air around them shattered.

"What the hell is this?" He waved the piece of paper in front of Rick as Rick's stomach tied in knots.

"Some of the classes I'm taking this semester."

"Some?" his voice raised, and Rick looked out the back of the truck. He saw two people waiting at the intersection, both of them watching the blow-up as cars honked at one another.

"It's no big deal. It's my first semester, and I'm trying to knock out my gen ed early is all," Rick said, knowing full well it wasn't the general education his grandfather had a problem with. He remembered how his grandpa fell apart when his grandma left.

Rick's grandma had abandoned the family a year prior, and his grandpa spent most of Rick's senior year preparing to sell the home they'd shared for four decades. Grandpa made him promise he would never let himself get to a point where he relied on someone else the way Grandpa relied on his wife.

"I don't think I can do this anymore," he confessed one night when Rick had finished his midterms, but when Rick went to hug him, his grandpa left his office and locked himself away in his room.

Rick snapped back to attention, realizing he hadn't heard the question his grandpa just asked. "Huh?"

"I *said*, what happened to business or engineering? I thought you even considered pre-med like your father. Music! You mean that stupid little hobby that keeps you busy when you should be working," he said.

"I just thought if I went to school for it, it wouldn't be a hobby anymore."

"Damn right it wouldn't. It'd be worse; you'd be in debt to it." He shook his head and crumpled the class schedule in his fist. "You're gonna fix this. Right now, you're gonna call the school and tell them there's been a mistake." The two boys came closer, and Rick stepped away from the desk.

"It's my education," Rick said.

"Then you can pay for it." He wagged a finger at his grandson.

"Fine, I will."

"And you can move out."

"Excuse me?"

"You want to study music, you can find your own place."

"You're kicking me out?"

"I'm teaching you a lesson. You have to be able to take care of yourself first. That should always be your top priority. If you really think music can do that for you, fine. I won't stop you, but you're gonna have to pay for school, room and board, books—all of it on your own."

"Okay," Rick said, but his voice faltered. He was adding up what he assumed some of the costs would be and knew that even with the financial aid the school offered, covering his own expenses would be near impossible. Not to mention, a small part of him knew his grandpa was right. What if he couldn't get a job with a music degree?

"Don't be stupid. Play drums in your free time, join a band if you can, but don't bet your entire life on a pipe dream."

"Instead, you think I should give up all my goals in life in favor of playing it safe."

His grandpa's nostrils flared. "What you call playing safe, I call responsible. There's nothing brave about taking a shot you know you're gonna miss. That Wayne Gretzky was a damn idiot, son. Only fools put all their eggs in one basket." Before Rick could respond, his grandpa added, "Even the rare few who succeed had to be foolish to get there. When your parents dropped you off at my house, they made me promise to protect you. That includes protecting you from your own stupid decisions. Have you ever stopped to think maybe these wrinkles on my face mean I've seen a thing or two and know what I'm talking about?" He grabbed the desk around its middle and lifted with his legs. It rose higher than Rick ever got it on his own, and he shuffled to the end of the truck and climbed down without dropping the desk.

Rick followed. The pit in his stomach tightened, and he wanted to say something—anything—but the words escaped his mind. He knew he wasn't wrong for wanting to play, but felt like maybe his grandpa had a point. Maybe he was wrong for dreaming about music all this time. Focusing on reality didn't make the dream any less enjoyable, and he could still find a way to play, but maybe betting his entire future on it was wrong.

"You know I'm right. I always am with you." His grandpa smirked, and Rick wasn't sure if he was joking or not. Still, Rick wanted to yank the corners of his mouth down. Grandpa wasn't always right, no matter how much he claimed he was.

"Is that why grandma left? She couldn't handle you always being right?" Rick knew he went too far the moment the words left his mouth. He got his wish; his grandpa's smile disappeared instantly, but the cold stare of the old man's brown eyes shot ice through Rick's veins. He shrunk back, but his grandpa was too fast, grabbing him by the wrist so tightly he worried it would snap off like a pretzel.

"Are you sure you want to go down that road, you little shit?" he never heard his voice sound like that before. His tone was icier than Buffalo in February. "Do you think you've been anything but a burden on our home since your parents dropped you off? Penny and I raised one kid already, if we wanted another, do you really think we would've waited til our sixties?" Spit skipped off his lips as he spoke down to his grandson. Rick winced as each drop hit his face, but he couldn't pull away.

The two boys who had been watching from the corner were only a few feet away now. Both had their phones out. Rick tried to hide his face behind his hand, but his grandpa grabbed him by his other wrist. "But despite how demanding you were, I kept my promise." Something changed in his grandpa's face. The harsh laugh lines around his grandpa's mouth looked born from cackles, and his brown eyes seemed to glow red like the Terminator.

The more he tried to pull his wrist away, the tighter his grandpa's grip got. He wanted to ask him to stop—to say he was hurting him and plead with his grandpa, maybe even apologize, but the two boys were only a few feet away with their phones out. What would they think seeing a teenager getting overpowered by a 70-year-old?

"Let go." Rick deepened his voice, trying to give an air of command.

"Apologize," his grandpa said.

Rick didn't want to hurt him, but he could hear the kids laughing. His grandpa could try to take away his dreams, but he couldn't take away his pride. Without warning, Rick twisted his body, wielding an open hand towards his grandpa's face. He closed his eyes, preparing for impact, when he felt a hard bone strike his forearm.

Opening his eyes and wincing, Rick yanked his hand away. His grandpa blocked his strike and, without hesitation, delivered his own open hand slap. The sound cracked through the air. At first, Rick didn't feel a thing, but as the sound disappeared, he finally felt the sting of the impact. The pain spread through his cheek. His face was burning, but before he could say another word, his grandpa shifted his weight, and—still holding Rick's wrist—leveraged his body so Rick flipped over his back and smacked against the pavement. He coughed and tried to breathe, but no air entered his lungs. His grandpa yanked him up by the collar, pinning his knee against Rick's gut. A narrow finger wagged in his face.

"If you talk about her like that one more time, your graduation gift will be finding a new place to live." He let Rick fall flat on the ground and returned to the desk. Rick closed his eyes, half from pain and half from embarrassment. He knew, without looking, those boys had captured the whole thing on video.

Chapter 5

With most of Lindsey's merchandise safely stored over at PackDaddy, she spent the next four weeks selling at a few local craft fairs at various community centers, which often had very low table fees. While the profits at those weren't amazing, she needed whatever cash she could get to subsidize her massive order for ArtCon. The local fairs went by slower. Lindsey worked tables alone since Athena never came to suburban craft fairs. Too many suburban moms would get offended at the nudity, and Athena was one of those high-brow artsy types who couldn't handle criticism. Lindsey's Punk Kitty enamel pins sold well with high schoolers in the burbs, so the more craft fairs she went to in their school gyms, the better. She was the Scholastic Books of kitty pins.

By mid-March, Lindsey had almost made back what she paid for the storage unit, and was optimistic she would make rent.

On a Sunday night in mid-March after a craft fair, Lindsey sat naked at her desk once again, staring at herself in the mirror. The image sent tingles up her spine—

nothing got her more high than her own naked body. She worked on some new drawings while listening to more Shawn Boston.

Lindsey desperately needed a relaxing evening. She was exhausted from today's fair, and the string of uncertainties that had recently entered her life were stressing her out. After successfully navigating the storage unit fiasco last month, Lindsey had gotten a few emails that all of her planned April and May craft fairs had been postponed due to the coronavirus. The virus was getting worse everywhere; doctors advised people to stay home when possible, and not to gather in groups of more than 50. Thankfully, Lindsey's recent events were on the smaller side, often in big rooms like community centers or school gyms, and rarely had more than 30 or so people there at a time. But all the upcoming mid-tier cons and spring street festivals expected bigger crowds, and they weren't considered safe. Some of them were able to refund Lindsey's deposit, but most couldn't.

At this point, Lindsey had to bank everything on ArtCon. She couldn't imagine the virus would still be this bad by July; someone would develop a vaccine or at the very least, the spread would slow down or die out, right? July was still four months away. Even if all her mid-tier spring festivals were canceled for April and May, she still had two Chicago street festivals in June to look forward to, then her big trip to New York in July for ArtCon.

She turned to Shawn Boston on YouTube—her new favorite source for chill music.

She was starting to become a fan of Shawn himself; she thought it was cool how Shawn apparently started from nothing and ended up making it big on YouTube.

As she started coloring in a new rainbow version of Punk Kitty to save for Pride Month social media graphics, she listened to a few of Shawn Boston's vlogs. In addition to making music videos, Shawn liked to talk about his own life, his day to day activities, and his stories of how he got here. Shawn had more vlogs than he had music videos, and Lindsey couldn't deny that they were interesting.

By the time she finished her art for the night, Lindsey had listened to 8 of Shawn's vlogs. She learned that he came from a small, middle-of-nowhere town in Indiana and moved to Los Angeles when he was 21 to pursue music. Shawn was 25 now and had spent the past four years working day and night to grow his music career up from nothing.

Lindsey didn't often feel inspired by other people's success; that was more Athena's thing. While Athena loved gurus like Elise Shiloh, Lindsey remained more skeptical. When she listened to Shawn's videos, she knew that he probably exaggerated at least some of his success. He probably did more than just move to LA, grind all day, and then become a breakout indie star. But regardless, he was able to do it.

In Shawn's most recent vlog, he discussed how he was planning to release a new album in a couple weeks. The album, called "Fruits of My Labor," was going to include a bunch of the songs from his YouTube channel, plus a few new ones that he hadn't released yet. In his vlogs, Shawn loved to show his behind-the-scenes process, including working in the recording studio with his friend and producer, Dave "D-Wagon" Williams.

The more Lindsey watched Shawn, the more she wondered if she really did need to get an online store set up. Shawn sold all his albums exclusively online. He'd never had one released as a CD or a record. He sold everything digitally. Plus, he made money on ad revenue from the corporate advertisements that played before his

YouTube videos. Shawn was a lot like Lindsey—a self-starting artist in his own way. But he used the internet to his advantage, and now he didn't have to worry about events being canceled the way Lindsey was.

Maybe, while her spring events were canceled, Lindsey could finally give all her time to this whole online store thing.

Lindsey woke up at noon, like she usually did on weekdays. Hey, when you're an artist who makes most of your money at conventions and festivals, weekends are the real work week, and Monday might as well be Saturday. Lindsey would've slept until 1 or 2 pm if not for her phone vibrating on her face. That's what she got for letting herself fall asleep with her cell phone on her pillow. She should've listened to all of her mom's 2003-era fears about cell phones putting weird radiation waves into your brain. If her mom had just framed the warning as "sleeping with the cell phone near your face might cause someone to call you, waking you up an hour before you want to," then maybe she would've listened the first time.

As it turned out, Lindsey's mom was the one calling. Lindsey sluggishly sat up.

"Mom?" she asked, her voice deep and groggy.

"Lindsey! Are you just waking up?"

"Yeah, the call woke me up."

Normally, when Lindsey said things like "your call woke me up," she expected the other person to apologize. As far as she knew, it was common courtesy to apologize for waking someone up. However, she also knew that this was her *mom* she was talking to, meaning remorse was a rare commodity.

"Well, it's a good thing I called then! It's almost noon!"

"You think it's a good thing you woke me up?"

"Yes, Lindsey. Did you miss the part when I said it's almost noon?"

"No, Mom, I heard you. Did you miss the million times I've told you that Mondays are my weekend? I worked 12 hours on my feet yesterday. How about, 'I'm sorry for waking you up, Lindsey.'"

"Well, maybe I wouldn't have woken you up if you would stop sleeping with your cell phone next to your face like you did back in high school. You're going to get radiation tumors one of these days--"

"Got it. Thanks Mom."

"I'm serious, Lindsey, I—"

"Why did you call?"

"I wanted to make sure you weren't planning to go to any new craft fairs. I know you like to do those, but this virus is really starting to concern me."

"Don't worry, Mom. All of my events are canceled at least through May. Yesterday was my last one."

"That's good to hear."

"It's good to hear that your daughter's main income source is gone?"

"Lindsey, I've told you so many times not to gamble on making all your money on art!"

"Until this virus started, I *had* been making a full-time income on art!"

"Lindsey, I hope you're not going to try to do more craft fairs in this virus..."

"I just said they've all been canceled."

"Well, I didn't know if you meant that for real. I keep hearing Tony using the word 'canceled' to just mean, like, when a celebrity isn't cool anymore. So, I didn't know if you were just using your young people slang to tell me that craft fairs aren't cool anymore."

"Do you really think I would stop going to craft fairs, which I just said were my primary source of income, just because they're not cool?"

"I don't know, Lindsey! You do a lot of things that make no logical sense. Like pursuing art, for one thing. You could've been just as good at consulting as Tony was. Better, even. You were always the one with that magnetic personality!"

"Which is why I'm good at sales. You know, at conventions."

"So why not get a job in sales?"

Lindsey stopped for a moment. No matter how much she wanted to just tell her mom to fuck off, she probably had a point. Lindsey's source of income was gone at least for the next few months. Lying in bed wasn't going to do anything about that. Until the online store went live, she'd at least have to find a job of some sort, right? If for no other reason than to placate Francisco.

"That's a good idea. I'll look for something." Lindsey said matter-of-factly, and hung up before her mom could say something smug like, "I know it's a good idea, otherwise I wouldn't have suggested it."

Lindsey got out of bed and decided to get dressed in somewhat professional clothes. She didn't own anything even approaching business casual, but she figured a black scoop-neck shirt was the best she could do, especially if she was going to head out to job search. She pulled on her only pair of jeans that didn't have holes in them and headed to her tiny bathroom to fix her hair.

Lindsey stared at her hair in the mirror as she waited for her flat-iron to heat up. A couple months ago, she'd put neon pink highlights in her shoulder-length dark brown hair. The pink highlights had been gradually fading, and she'd ordered some more dye off of Amazon to re-do them. But now, she thought as she began straightening her hair, it was probably good that they'd faded into her hair, looking like natural reddish-brown highlights from the sun. If she was really going to attempt to get a regular job today, the more natural her hair looked the better.

Lindsey searched "sales jobs near me" on her phone, and a variety of results instantly popped up. A jewelry store the next neighborhood over. A high-end clothing shop a couple blocks away. An electronics store a mile south.

After making a quick paper cup full of coffee from the lobby Keurig machine, Lindsey headed out the door and toward, hopefully, a potential day job opportunity. First, she tried the clothing store a couple blocks away.

She opened the door to Clothes Galore and stepped inside. Heavy potpourri scents assaulted her nose . She looked around at racks and racks of fancy-looking suit jackets and button-down shirts. She looked down at her own shirt, which covered most of her boobs, but not enough for this place. She knew she wasn't going to fit in here.

"Oh my god, what are you doing?" a woman in a white pantsuit and matching silk face mask asked.

"Oh, I saw online that you—"

"You need to wear a mask in this store! We can NOT have you getting coronavirus all over the clothes!"

"Oh. Sorry."

Lindsey turned around and darted out the door. There was no way she was going to get the job after that.

Before Lindsey got on the bus to check out the jewelry or electronics stores, she decided she'd need to get a hold of a face mask. She had noticed people wearing masks more frequently, but she didn't know they were becoming a necessity so quickly. She stopped at a drugstore on the street corner and bought a plain black cloth mask to cover her nose and mouth.

Walking out of the drugstore with her new mask on, she briefly caught a glimpse of her reflection in the window. With her nose and mouth covered, her already lacking look had plummeted to downright unprofessional. She was worried that if she entered a jewelry store or an electronics store dressed in all black like she was, with her face covered, she'd be taken for a burglar. But if everyone was wearing masks, what could she do? Lindsey made a mental note to get some clothes—other than pajamas or hand-me-downs she stole from Chad—that weren't black.

She hopped on the next bus heading south and found herself in a sea of other people in face masks, though not everyone had one on. She took a seat next to an elderly woman wearing a bandana over her nose and mouth. If this virus really was spreading so fast that everyone had to wear masks—even if they didn't have it—then maybe riding the public bus wasn't the best idea right now. But she was already here, and she needed a job.

When Lindsey entered the electronics store, she was glad to see that no one was dressed as upscale as they were at Clothes Galore. This store was part of the first-floor retail in a larger apartment complex. Flat-screen TVs were on display in the window, and on the door was a sign saying that the Nintendo Switch was sold out.

Inside the store, a chubby man with a beard greeted her. "Hi, how can I help you?" he asked. His beard was so long that even though he was wearing a bandana as his facial covering—like the lady on the bus—his beard hairs were still visible, peeking out from the bottom.

"I saw online that you have openings for sales jobs. I

was wondering if I could interview—"

"Oh, is that listing still up?"

"...Yes?"

"Silly me! I should've taken that down last week. We sold out of the Nintendo Switch, and most people are looking for their other electronics online right now, so we don't actually have the opening anymore. Sorry."

"Thanks anyway."

Next, Lindsey took the bus to the jewelry store, only to find the door completely boarded up. "CLOSED FOR COVID," it read.

Well, this was a waste of time—and a waste of potentially exposing herself to the virus on all these bus trips.

She headed back home and decided, just for the heck of it, to stop in the restaurants, grocery stores, and cafes on her own block. Those places were still operating, right? People still had to eat!

But each one told her the same thing: they could barely afford to keep their doors open right now, let alone hire someone new. Some of them had even laid off employees.

The corner store manager gave her the most thorough explanation: "Everybody's lost their job to covid right now. So, no one has money. Which means no one has money to shop here. And when people *do* shop here for food, they get only the basics. A lot of people are trying to buy food online. We're barely going to make rent, let alone hire someone new."

Completely dejected, Lindsey entered her own apartment building once again.

<hr />

After a week of watching her bank account deplete, plus a few days of Francisco angrily stopping her on the elevator to remind her that he had the power to evict her whenever he wanted, Lindsey decided she needed to try the online store thing. It was still 3 months until her next event, and almost 4 months until ArtCon, and the bills weren't going to pay themselves 'til then.

On a Friday evening at the end of March, Lindsey sat at her computer with Athena on the couch next to her. Athena had ordered enough Thai takeout to feed a small army, which she'd placed carefully across Lindsey's floor so she could spread out her art supplies on the coffee table in front of her.

"How are you planning to make rent this month?" Lindsey asked, swiveling around in her desk chair, sporting Chad's old XXL sweatshirt and a pair of leggings. Athena was thankful that Lindsey put clothes on whenever she came downstairs to visit, even if sometimes it was just a sports bra and underwear.

Athena opened her sketchbook on Lindsey's coffee table and selected one of her fancy graphite pencils. She began sketching. "What do you mean?"

"Well, you haven't done a festival with me since CreateCon over a month ago. And all our events until at least June have been canceled. I'm seriously running out of money."

"Have you considered getting a sugar daddy?" Athena asked, completely straight-faced.

"Is that a joke?"

"No. You flirt with guys to sell to them at conventions. Why not take the next step?"

"Is that what *you're* doing to make rent?" Lindsey asked.

"No, of course not. Not entirely."

"What do you mean by—"

"Also, my grandma sent me $5,000 for Christmas so I'm still working through that."

Sometimes Lindsey forgot that Athena was blessed with Rich Grandma Privilege.

Lindsey turned back to her computer screen, where she had been working on setting up a page on ShopNow. While she worked and while Athena drew, one of Shawn Boston's new songs played in the background.

"Who's this music? I like it," Athena said.

"It's Shawn Boston. I found him on YouTube. His songs are pretty cool. This one's from his new album that's releasing next week."

"Oh, I think I've heard of him. Elise Shiloh has featured him on her blog a few times."

Lindsey nodded. "That makes sense, with Shawn being a self-starter and everything."

Athena sketched a large, voluptuous woman. Next to her, she began outlining a man, who was dangling grapes to feed her. "This piece is going to be the sequel to *Grape Nipples*," Athena said. "It's going to be called *Grape Love*."

Lindsey nodded, a little jealous that Athena could just focus so hard on the integrity of her art all the time rather than making sales. She wondered how she could get Athena's rich grandma to adopt her.

Lindsey clicked the big red "launch" button in the corner of the ShopNow site , and there it was: PunkKitty-ByLindseyDrake.com was live.

"What do people do now?" Lindsey asked. "Once they set up online stores, I mean? Do they just wait for sales to come in?"

Athena shrugged, not looking up from her sketches on the coffee table. She drew another thick line, letting the graphite coat the outside of her right hand as it dragged across the page. "I don't sell online. How would I possibly know?"

"Well, I figured, since you've read Elise Shiloh's blog

and her business advice and such."

"Oh," said Athena, drawing another thick line across the page. "I took Elise Shiloh's course about sales pitching face-to-face. Her online marketing advice is an entire separate course."

It was astounding how Elise could sell so much specialized information in differently packaged courses and make so much money from it. Lindsey briefly wondered if she was in the wrong business, being an artist.

While Athena took a break from drawing to shove a yarn ball-sized clump of Thai noodles into her mouth, Lindsey searched for Elise Shiloh's internet selling advice. When she reached the front page of her blog, she saw a familiar face—Shawn Boston.

"Elise Shiloh is proud to serve as the art curator for Shawn Boston's new album cover!" the page read.

"Oh, that's cool," Lindsey said. "Did you know Elise was part of the cover design process for Shawn's new album?"

"That's really cool," Athena said, her words muffled through a mouthful of pad Thai. "What does the album art look like?"

"No one knows yet. He's not revealing the art until the date of the album drop. It's some big mystery."

"That's really cool," Athena agreed.

"Well, I guess all I can do now is sit here and wait to make a sale," Lindsey said. As Lindsey closed the ShopNow tab on her laptop and went to sit next to Athena on the couch, she saw a notification pop up on her phone —an email from ArtCon.

She gulped nervously, then tapped the email, hoping her worst fears weren't about to come true. After a deep breath, she read the subject line:

"ArtCon 2020 Cancelled Due to Coronavirus."

Chapter 6

Rick texted Rufus the next morning asking if he needed help before they opened. He typed out "I'm sorry" a dozen ways, including Spanish, but couldn't bring himself to hit send. His resolve softened when he thought of Rufus pressing his hands together and his thick mustache wiggling to hide a trembling lip, but the moment Rick remembered feeling the warm spotlight on his face, its heat raising his heart rate. But the thought of typing an apology now made him feel dirty. He went to wash his hands, and before he could dry them off, he felt his phone buzz.

"Hello?" he finally answered after the third swipe, fumbling to quickly wipe his hands on his shorts. He'd never received a call from his boss before noon.

"Hey kid, I'm glad you reached out. I was meaning to talk to ya when you came in."

This was it, Rick thought, squeezing his phone. He needed to help his grandpa pay for rent and he couldn't even bring himself to fake an apology to his boss—how could he work in a comedy club and not be able to lie?

"I know it was unfair to put you on the spot like that," Rufus continued. Suddenly, Rick's phone slipped from his hands, still wet from his half-assed attempt at drying them. The phone landed on the bed, and Rick could no longer make out what Rufus was saying. Desperate to hear, Rick dropped to the bed and lowered his head close to the phone. He tried to press "Speaker" but his wet hands glided off the screen and couldn't get enough pressure to signal to the way-too-expensive cheap piece of shit that he needed it to speak louder.

"Come on," Rick groaned. He finally managed to put the phone on speaker when he wiped his finger on the blanket and pressed the button again.

"You there?" Rufus asked.

"Yep! Yep, I'm here," Rick replied quickly. *Fucking touch screens*, he thought to himself.

"Well, that's pretty much all I have to say. Thanks again kid," he said and hung up.

It could've gone worse. It's not like he chewed Rick out, and he sounded apologetic at the end. Whatever Rufus had said, Rick was sure he could recover somehow on his shift that night.

The day flew by. He spent most of it listening to music in his room and scrolling through videos on YouTube. He rolled his eyes when he saw Shawn Boston was releasing a new album. Just what the world needed: another trash album from a trash internet celebrity.

There was no cover art next to the title, but the description sounded halfway between pompous and brain dead—like something an angsty zombie might write as he promised to connect with his fans on a deeper level than they ever had before. The world was a better place when the forums were debating whether or not Shawn would cut his hair.

How did someone as basic as Shawn Boston get so lucky? He probably never actually had to struggle a day in his life. Why was it endearing when he made online confessions, but Rick had to endure dubstep remixes and dramatized re-enactments of his fight with his grandpa? Shawn could scare off Girl Scouts trying to sell him cookies and the internet would laugh with him at those stupid little kids, but Rick couldn't even buy a box without the girls pulling up a video and asking if that was really him.

As he finally left for work that evening, he was relieved to see the apartment was empty. He didn't know or care where his grandpa was; he couldn't face another confrontation. Rick hopped in place with his arms buried in his coat as he waited at the bus stop, and was pleasantly surprised when the bus actually arrived on time. No one else was on the bus, either; he was able to lean back and prop his feet up.

The parking lot at Low Octave was almost completely empty, but that was normal for early evening on an open mic night. The crowd never picked up until after dinner, when the late-night drink specials kicked in for people who weren't finding their warm tingles from the punchlines on stage.

Rick approached the front door, realizing as he got closer that the lights weren't on. As the sun began to set, the building's blue facade faded to black—the multistory buildings surrounding it still glowed orange above him, reflecting just enough light that Rick could see his breath. He tried for the door, but it wouldn't budge. He was about to call Rufus to ask what was going on when he saw the white sign on the board with the abstract circular icon of Low Octave stamped on the bottom:

Due to growing concerns of COVID-19

Low Octave is postponing all remaining shows for the
week.
Stay safe,
Low Octave

Rick tried the door again. He couldn't believe it. Why
wouldn't Rufus bother to let staff know they were closing
for the week? Why hadn't he just quit yesterday like he
wanted to? Rick was suddenly overcome with an emotion
he couldn't identify. It wasn't just anger; it had to be more,
like the feeling was always there and just ready to present
itself. It felt more like instinct in a sharp red pantsuit. He
pulled his phone out, ready to yell Rufus' stupid mustache
off his face, when he remembered the call that morning.
The conversation he missed because he couldn't get his
phone to work. Leaning against the glass door, he slid to
the ground and bounced his head back. The thump of his
head against the wall kicked off a beat, which he continued
with his fingers on his knees.

Why did this always happen? Even when things felt like
they were starting to go his way, the little things fell
through the cracks. Looking back to the road, he knew he
had a thirty minute wait until the next bus arrived,
assuming it was on time, and he couldn't afford to get a
ride if he wanted to help with rent. He certainly couldn't
kill time at one of the bars with the overpriced beers, so he
started north and walked home in silence.

The drumsticks slipped through his stiff fingers again. No
matter how much he flexed his hands, the cold was still in
his bones. Sniffling, he pulled out his phone and called
Genie.

"Yo-ho!"

"You sound peppy," Rick replied, sliding onto the basement floor, and tucking his knees under his shirt. His arms hugged all his body heat together. "Having a good day?"

"Not really. We think we're going into a lockdown soon. The streets are quiet and I'm too nervous to get groceries."

"Really? Over COVID?" He stopped himself from saying more. All he had to complain about was not getting a couple shifts this week. "Are you okay?" He wanted to teleport through the phone and sit beside her, even if she turned out to be the black wall she looked like on his screen.

"I don't know, I'm nervous, especially about my parents. You know my dad has asthma and they're saying we need to keep our distance from high risk people so I doubt I can even check in on them." Her voice cracked; she had no sarcastic remarks. For the first time since they met more than five years ago, they sat in silence.

"That's awful. Is there anything I can do?" He already knew the answer, but he needed to feel like he could help her, be there for her—do something. Instead, he felt trapped on the cold concrete basement floor.

"Have you been recording any music?" Genie asked. Rick could tell she wanted to steer the conversation away from herself. It wasn't a surprise. In the half decade they'd been friends, he had only seen her face a dozen times. She carefully curated how she was seen in any interaction with friends, something Rick never fully understood. He wanted to prove he was the kind of friend she could be entirely open with, but he assumed she found comfort in concealing her problems. Like confidence could be as consistent as an avatar on the screen.

"Ha, you're funny," he replied, slapping a cymbal with

his hand. The cold metal stung his skin on impact. "Closest I'll ever get to that are these private shows for you."

"Good thing I'm recording it then," Genie chuckled.

"Very funny." Rick rolled his eyes and scooped up his drumsticks, climbing back onto the drum set stool. If she was about to mess with him, he could drown her out with a steady beat.

"What do you think of Big Rick Energy?" she asked before he started playing.

"I think it's good for a t-shirt, but you better not put my face on it."

"Nah, just your YouTube channel."

"My what?" the hair on his forearms stood on end. She couldn't be serious. She knew everything he'd gone through; no way would she make him a channel. But sure enough, when he searched Big Rick Energy on YouTube, the first channel to pop up had a picture of him and one subscriber. "What the hell's your problem?"

"What do you mean? You said work's out for at least a week. You need something to do," she said, but Rick was already looking for ways to delete the account. It would've helped if she'd given him the password to a channel with his name and face on it, but apparently that was too much to ask. "Just sleep on it," Genie added.

She hung up before he could respond. Rick held his breath as he clicked the video. Of course, the quality was low, she had recorded one of their video calls on her phone. The sound was slightly garbled, and under the dim basement light he could barely make himself out—his face was grainy, and his hoodie hid most of his frame. Still, he couldn't ignore the profile picture Genie used for his channel. It was from a few years ago, around the time his video went viral. If there were ever a photo that could turn the spotlight of the world back on him it was that. He had no idea how to log into the account; he wasn't even sure what email Genie used. Following her advice, Rick went upstairs to bed.

Rick struggled to sleep all night. He kept imagining his phone sparking into a massive fire that spread up the walls of his room. The flames flashed like camera bulbs and lit the night like fireworks, burning off his clothes. He leapt for safety, but the crowd under the building all had their phones out. Not a single hand raised to catch him, not a single phone budged. Their eyes all blended into one lens when he smacked against the pillow and woke up with a pool of drool sticking to his cheek.

He needed to see the video. Genie probably just ruined his life. It was only a matter of time until he was back on everyone's profile as the loser who lost a fight to "random old man" or "some old guy." The "kid gets owned by grandpa" brand was coming back to the internet and there was nothing he could do to stop it. It was all Genie's fault. What was she thinking? He pulled YouTube back up on his phone. wincing from both the screen brightness and the impending . How many people could've found him overnight? He supposed anyone having a bad day would be excited to laugh at him again, but when he found his channel, his heart leapt. He still only had one subscriber, Genie, and his video had 2 views. They could've both been him for all he knew. It was possibly the first time he ever smiled at his phone while his own face was on the screen. Before, the device had been nothing but a window into the most embarrassing moment of his life, but maybe he could return to it; maybe he didn't have to be faceless the rest of his life.

Without the numbers piling on the video, he listened to

it again, and this time he noticed the recommended videos listed below. They were filled with ideas for songs he could cover; he could even record a session over popular music. He could do anything once (or rather, *if*) the world finally forgot who he was.

Chapter 7

Lindsey didn't allow herself to wallow in the misery of ArtCon being cancelled. She told herself she had to think positively, like that Elise Shiloh pamphlet Athena made her read. She had to move forward. If all she did was worry about where her next paycheck was coming from, well... that wasn't going to make it magically appear, now was it?

In the three days since ArtCon had been cancelled, Lindsey's online store had made a total of two sales. She'd shipped out the enamel pins to her customers, trying to provide good customer service, but it sucked that her total sales for the week were literally less than $50. This wasn't going to be sustainable.

Trying to brainstorm some ideas, Lindsey sat down at her computer the Friday after ArtCon had been canceled —the night before Shawn Boston's album was supposed to drop—and headed to YouTube for some inspiration. Shawn made all his money online and documented every step of the way—there had to be something she could learn from that.

Maybe she needed to be just a little bit like E-Thot McGee—after all, she, and Shawn both had YouTube channels and were both successful. If Lindsey could gain fans on her own YouTube channel, that had to help with online sales. But Lindsey never wanted to be one of those artists who spent all her time working on content marketing and promotions for her work instead of the art itself. But how else could she survive the pandemic? The art itself wasn't paying the bills.

Lindsey logged onto YouTube and clicked the "create account" button. There was still a way to keep it all about the art, right? She could just make videos about drawing; she didn't have to make vlogs about her daily life. She could make drawing tutorials using screen recordings of her Punk Kitty design process, and leave links to her store in the description of each video like other YouTubers did. It was the perfect way to funnel customers without paying money for ads.

Lindsey created her brand-new YouTube channel: PunkKittyByLindseyDrake, to match the website. For her profile picture, she decided on a photo of herself from CreateCon holding up a piece of her art in a low-cut black top that showed off her cleavage—emulating E-Thot McGee's marketing style.

Next, she uploaded a header image, which was the same image she used for her booth banners at festivals. Recording videos was surprisingly easy; all she had to do was screen record the work she was already doing. As she drew her latest design, she watched the new vlog from Shawn Boston: "Get Ready with Me for My New Album Drop." Shawn walked around his large LA home, where he had his own recording studio next to the living room, and showed footage of himself and Dave "D-Wagon" Williams working on the album. Then, Shawn cut back to the present as he posed in his walk-in closet, trying on outfits to find one for the launch. Lindsay looked around at her tiny apartment, with its broken doorknob and old, flat carpet; she had never felt smaller.

When her new piece was done, she stopped her recording software and saved the new video file. She found some stock ukulele music online, layered that music under her video, and prepared the new file to upload.

She titled her video "How to Draw a Cat," tagged it as "art," then waited for the views to roll in.

Only they didn't roll in. When Lindsey checked back on her video three hours later, it had just two views—and she was one of them.

But what she did have more of, though, was art video recommendations in her YouTube feed. One channel looked particularly intriguing: the DrawmaLlamas. Their video was called "Drawing Elise Shiloh, Scammer Supreme."

Interesting. Lindsey knew Athena was a big fan of Elise, but Lindsey had always gotten a bit of a scammer vibe from her, even though she was friends with Shawn. Plus, this was an art channel, so that had to mean something.

In the video, a man, and a woman—who called them-selves the DrawmaLlamas— recorded their screen while drawing just like Lindsey had done. Neither showed their face, and both talked using only voiceover to accompany the drawing. While they talked, lines for their drawing of Elise slowly appeared.

The two of them roasted Elise hard, talking about how her courses were a scam, charging hundreds or even thou-sands of dollars to teach very basic sales principles. The woman mentioned that one of her friends, who was a busi-ness major, had taken Elise's course but learned more in her Business 101 textbook freshman year—and that book cost less than a tenth of Elise's course.

Throughout the nearly half-hour-long video, the DrawmaLlamas drew a complete picture of Elise, colored her in, and shit-talked her to no end. The video had nearly a million views. Lindsey's video was now at three views.

As Lindsey looked through her feed of recommended videos after watching the DrawmaLlamas, she realized that videos trash-talking celebrities and influencers got more views than anything else she'd ever seen.

Videos that discussed "drama" or "spilling the tea" or "exposing people" got hundreds of thousands, if not millions, of views. And the DrawmaLlamas did all of this while creating art.

In the description of the DrawmaLlamas' video about Elise, Lindsey saw their website linked: DrawmaLlamas.com. They boasted tons of merch—including enamel pins and patches like Lindsey sold—featuring llamas.

So, this is how they do it, Lindsey thought. They grab people's attention by trash talking popular people online, then use that attention to sell their art.

It was brilliant.

But it also seemed wrong in a way. Lindsey didn't join YouTube to expose people or to spill about drama. She was hoping to promote her art and her business, but she didn't really *want* to join YouTube. She just thought it was a good marketing technique.

Lindsey spent the next 4 hours bingeing all of the DrawmaLlamas' videos while drinking her way through a box of white wine. Most of them had at least a couple hundred thousand views.

She decided to play a drinking game with herself: drink every time someone in the comment section mentioned that they were so glad they'd found the DrawmaLlamas' channel and talked about how they'd bought llama merch or art from their website. She was drunk as a skunk after two videos.

By the time Lindsey had finished watching all of the DrawmaLlamas' videos, she had finished the entire box.

Lindsey closed her laptop and stumbled over to her bed, which was a hot mess of laundry. She flopped down, naked, across the piles of clothes and stared at the ceiling.

It was a Friday night and Lindsey was alone in her apartment. Before this pandemic hit, Friday nights were for first days of conventions or preparing for Saturday craft fairs. Friday nights were for preparing to make money. Fridays were when Lindsey's real work week started. But now, there was no work, and there was no week, and Lindsey had no money.

The next morning, Lindsey fished around the laundry piles for a bra, put on the first one she found, and then squeezed her giant chest into her old My Chemical Romance T-shirt from high school. She found some pajama pants and some flip-flops, then headed toward the elevator.

Lindsey felt like trash, so it was a good morning to get some coffee from the apartment lobby's Keurig machine. The Keurig machine always made the coffee nice and strong, and Lindsey's head was pounding—partially from her hangover, and partially from the stress of her lack of sales.

When she reached the lobby, she walked over to the counter with the Keurig machine, pulled a coffee pod out of the drawer, and got a paper cup out of the cabinet below. Right as her coffee was pouring into the cup, creating a comforting, aromatic cloud of steam around her, she heard footsteps.

"Lindsey! What are you doing?"

She turned around to see Francisco, wearing just a white tank top and athletic shorts, storming towards her, pumping his short arms, his face scrunched up and beet red behind a medical-style mask.

"Just making coffee."

"You'd better disinfect that machine! I don't want germs spreading throughout our building!"

"I don't have the coronavirus," Lindsey said.

"I don't care what you think you have or don't think you have! From now on, you use the Clorox wipes to clean the machine every time you use it. And you wear a mask in the lobby!"

Lindsey hadn't realized how quickly the virus had been progressing; getting drunk alone in your apartment all day will do that to you.

"Okay, Francisco," she said.

"Do you know what today is, Lindsey?" His golden cross bounced on his barrel chest as he interrogated her aggressively.

"Uh, Saturday?"

"Yes! But it is the last Saturday of the month! You owe me for March rent."

"I'll get it to you. Just give me a few days." Lindsey quickly tried to do some math calculations in her head. "I can get you half by tomorrow."

"And when can you get me the other half?"

If she could just get a few sales up—if she could just gain some traction from her channel—"Maybe in a couple weeks?"

Francisco's eyes narrowed.

"I promise I can make it up at the end of April!"

"I expect both months' rent in full by the end of April or else you're out of here!" he yelled, pointing his giant index finger at Lindsey's face, and then storming out of the lobby.

Lindsey did as she was told, wiping down the Keurig machine with the Clorox wipes in the cabinet, then headed back up to her apartment with her paper cup full of steaming coffee.

She sat down at her desk and logged back onto YouTube. Her video was now up to 10 views. She even had one comment, which said "cute kitty." Okay, so at least this whole online thing was working a little bit. She just needed to figure out what to do for her next video—and it definitely had to be something more eye-catching than "how to draw a cat."

When Lindsey clicked back to the YouTube homepage, she saw a new video from Shawn Boston: "My New Album Launch!"

Lindsey clicked on the video and started to watch.

Shawn spoke to the camera, holding his acoustic guitar in his lap, profusely thanking his fans for making this new album, "Fruits of My Labor," possible. Then, he announced excitedly, it was time to reveal the album cover.

The new album cover popped up on the screen.

Lindsey froze. Her eyes grew wide. For a moment, she had to pause and consider whether what she was seeing in front of her was real.

Shawn's new album cover featured a naked woman lying in fruit. She was fully topless, her nipples covered with grapes. In each hand she held a glass of wine. At the top, Shawn Boston's name was splashed in giant all-caps letters. At the bottom was his album title, "Fruits of My Labor."

It should have said "Grape Nipples."

That, clear as day, was Athena's art on Shawn's cover.

Chapter 8

G enie finally gave Rick the login credentials to his
channel, though he still hadn't posted anything new.
He also didn't take down the first video, despite the sound
quality hitting his ears like a fork on a ceramic plate.

"You've been recording all week. Just post one already,"
Genie insisted during that night's phone call from the basement. All the videos on his phone were worse than the one
Genie posted. At least he could feel something when he
watched that one. Even though he couldn't see much, and
the sound quality was trash, his happiness from jamming
out translated through the screen with each strike against
the drumheads. His new stuff took that fun away. He
looked rigid, hitting the drum off beat because of the delay
from his background track. The music he was drumming
over was either so loud it made everything staticky, or just
quiet enough to make Rick's mistakes stand out.

"The longer you put off uploading, the scarier it's
gonna be," Genie added.

"Or I just don't want to put up crap," Rick replied. His
first video was still under ten views, and he knew that each

time he uploaded something new, he was opening himself to the possibility of being discovered again. Even if people liked his music, how long would it take for them to get from his page to the viral video? How long until the algorithm started recommending that embarrassing clip next to his new ones? And once they found out about his grandpa beating him up, would they care about his music, or would he stay a joke?

"Do you want to make music or not?"

"Of course I do," Rick replied.

"Then you're gonna have to put yourself out there," Genie replied.

Back in the apartment, Rick's grandpa was nowhere to be found. Talk of a potential lockdown in the city was spreading all over social media. He even saw rumors online of the National Guard getting called in. They were low on groceries and if they had to lockdown, who knew how long they would be trapped in the apartment together. Even if one of them killed the other, he doubted their meat would last long.

"Are you listening to me?" Genie cut in as he checked the fridge.

"Yeah, yeah, just—shit how long have you been locked down for?"

She went silent for a second. The white circle around her avatar disappeared, not even picking up on her breathing. "You there?"

"Like a week."

He marked down everything they needed and started for the corner store. If his grandpa wasn't going to let him help more with the rent, he could get food. Genie stayed on the phone while he shopped, always bringing the conversation back to music.

"You should be using this time to record," she noted as

he grabbed a loaf of bread.

"No one's gonna recognize you," she reassured as he walked toward the dairy aisle.

He wanted to believe her, and deep down he felt like she was right. It had been months since anyone at the bar brought it up to him.

As he finished shopping, he saw a red clearance sign over a stand-alone rack stocked with party decorations. There were red hearts, four leaf clovers, American flag-emblazoned top hats, and four sealed plastic bags with different costume titles labeled on the front of them. A rubber wolf mask stared down at him, and two clawed hands reached out from their wall perch.

"Uh, I gotta go. I'll call you when I get back to the apartment."

He walked around the clearance rack to the checkout counter where a teenage girl with acne and braces stood behind the register. As Rick unloaded his food from the basket, she began to giggle. The eggs, the milk, the butter, the giggling. She pulled out her phone and her smile grew too large for her face. Each chuckle was punctuated by a slurp.

Rick's gut tightened. Each laugh felt like another punch to his stomach, and as she turned her phone to show him the screen, he knew the question before "is that you?" left her lips. Sure enough, he saw himself five years younger and 30 pounds skinnier swinging at his grandpa, who threw him to the ground with ease. "Oh my god it is, right? It has to be. I mean the hair and the—you gained some weight, huh?"

All at once Rick knew why he couldn't keep recording music. At least not as himself. He was ink in water; no matter how little he touched it, he spread.

In his first YouTube video, the lighting and video

quality was shitty enough that no one could tell he was the same guy from the meme. However, if he started building the channel he would need better lighting, and sooner or later someone would be able to tell it was him. Unless... He looked back at the clearance rack.

"Wait, wait, can I please get a selfie?" The cashier started to come around and Rick backed up.

"Keep your distance," he said, and to his surprise, she listened. It had never worked before, and for the briefest of moments he wanted to thank COVID.

He left the store without a selfie, though he was sure the cashier took a number of pictures of him on his way out. He pulled his hoodie up trying to block his face, but the world felt like the eye of a lens now and anywhere he looked someone could snap a shot. His face would be safe soon, though. The answer was in his bag, and it was so simple. He just needed to wear a mask. He didn't know why he didn't think of it before. Even Genie hid herself behind an avatar online. It was all about the music; people wouldn't care if he wore a mask as long as they liked the songs.

He couldn't remember the last time he was excited to go online. His palms were sweating, and his heart fluttered when he made it back to his apartment. His grandpa still wasn't there. Where could he be? He was the one who brought up lockdowns; he mentioned that Sven's family was entering one.

After putting everything away, he went into his room and took out his new wolf mask. It smelled like plastic and cleaning solution; there was no way he could put it on yet.

The scent clogged his nose and made his throat tense up. He sent a selfie to Genie, then headed to the bathroom sink and started cleaning it as best as he could. Each scrub scratched a shade of regret into the gray rubber. If he was going to such measures to not be seen online, why do it at all?

"That's rock AF!" Genie texted back, approving of Rick's new wolf fur-sona. He wondered if she was being sarcastic. He finally heard the front door open and saw his grandpa walking in with a wide grin stretched across his face. He looked like the girl at the corner store; Rick chewed his bottom lip. Rick left his room to meet his grandpa in the kitchen.

His grandpa began to whistle as he grabbed a container of ice cream from the freezer and started eating out of the pint.

"Oh good, you're back. I was about to call you," his grandpa said. "Things are getting kinda serious out there right now. I think you should call into work and ask for some time off."

"Well, not much to worry about there. The club is closed for at least a week."

"Want a bite?" he held out the spoon and Rick winced. "Oh, come on. You can grab a bowl if you'd like."

Rick didn't say anything, so his grandpa continued. "Thanks for getting groceries. That was a good call."

"So, are we really going into lockdown?" Rick asked.

"I wouldn't be surprised," he sighed and put the ice cream on the counter. "I'm sorry for the way I snapped earlier." Rick stood back, skeptical. "It's just whenever we bring up your parents—my so- son," his lip trembled and he leaned forward with his elbows on his knees, burying his face in his hands. Rick crouched in front of him and put his hand on the veiny back of his grandfather's. Neither made a sound, letting the quietness wrap around them like a flannel comforter.

His grandpa pulled away first, wiping his bottom lip and reaching for the television remote. "They made me promise to look after you, is all. I can't imagine what they would think if I failed them to the point that you had to take care of me."

Rick squeezed his grandpa's shoulder and put the ice cream away. He heard an anchor announce breaking news on the television and knew the next statement would be anything but breaking.

In the basement, Rick rested his phone against his old business textbooks. At least they were getting some use now. Covered in sweat, and struggling to breathe from the chemical smell of the rubber wolf mask, he played his heart out. After a couple hours of jamming, he uploaded the recordings to his channel. Who could possibly pick him out now? He grabbed his laptop to surf online while he waited for his phone to upload the clips. It was taking forever, but he imagined the laptop would sound like an asthmatic marathon runner if he'd used it to upload a file even half the size.

SHAWN BOSTON ALBUM RELEASE! The text blinked across his screen the second he went online. He had never enjoyed Shawn's music, or videos, or face really, but the cover art looked different from anything he'd put out before. Maybe he was turning a new leaf. However, the second he played the first track and heard that overdone autotune bouncing against his eardrums like a deflated basketball, he knew he made a mistake. How could he think someone like Shawn Boston, whose greatest musical accomplishment was plucking knots from his hair, could actually create something worth listening to? It was less music and more a Twitter thread over an 808, with some bizarre string choices that Rick knew were meant to make kids lose their minds; it made him want to step out of his body just to slap himself silly. He skimmed through the rest of it, needing to know without a shadow of a doubt that the world was unfair and assholes like Shawn Boston would only trip on their face if it was into a million dollars. Jumping back to the YouTube homepage, he saw all of Shawn's most popular videos. Why was it so brave for *him* to confess to embarrassing moments or make a fool of himself on stream, but Rick couldn't even buy groceries without getting laughed at over something that happened five years ago?

All the comments were praising him:

"A genius!"

"We don't deserve Shawn!"

"If you don't like this you don't have ears!"

Compared to even the most flattering of Rick's comments: "LOL tool."

He typed out responses to these stupid teens, ready to put them in their stupid place, but couldn't bring himself to hit enter. "*You only think that becau*—" No, that's dumb. He kept typing until the comment turned into a wall of text, and he knew he'd look like a psycho if he sent it.

His phone buzzed, yanking his attention from the screen. "Yes!!!!!!" Genie texted him, and Rick grinned. The videos were up, and he actually had comments. Of course,

Genie's were at the top, making up 10 of the 13 current comments." Rick liked each of them before coming down to an avatar icon of the band name he included in the title. The group whose song he drummed over for the video.

"Is this some kinda furry shit?"

The comment under it wasn't much better. "They aren't for furries—" followed by a slur.

Rick knew never to go to the comment section; whatever was said in the video was multiplied by a thousand in the comments. It wasn't even a debate; it was as much a fact as wide right or forward lateral. What he didn't expect were comments to show up so quickly for an unknown channel. It's not like the first video got any views, but as he thought it through and looked back at the avatars, he realized two things at once: if he drummed over existing artists people were going to find him, and drumming online could actually work.

Genie called him and as soon as he answered she screamed. "You did it! You did it! I can't believe you did it!"

"You liked it then?"

"Still a little too raw, you gotta improve your quality. But it's a start dude! It's a start!"

They talked about the possibility of Rick growing some kind of audience online and all the possibilities it could create. He could possibly buy a new computer and a drum pad.

"You could be like Shawn Boston."

"Why did you have to bring him up?" He put his phone down and laid back on his bed. "Have you heard his new album?"

"Not yet, don't get the appeal, but the money sounds

nice."

Rick felt warm. "He fucking sucks," he said, feeling more energized as the words came out of his mouth. Finally, someone who saw that pretty boy for what he was.

"I wouldn't say that," Genie replied, and the energy rush deflated.

"Really? I thought given your symphonic taste you'd almost be insulted by how little effort he puts in. I couldn't even tell it was him singing. They layered it so much it could've been a feral cat screeching for food."

"Now you're just being mean," Genie chided. She wasn't wrong, but Rick scrunched his nose. It didn't matter if he was being mean; it's not like it made him any less right. Besides, Shawn had enough people being nice to him. Why was the world always willing to completely reshape itself for the comfort of these pretty pukes and no one else? If he put out a similar album, no one would have a single nice word to say about it.

Even now, he opened his YT Studio app and saw more comments pouring in, and almost all of them mentioned the mask. To his surprise, only one person hit the dislike button. Not the usual hailstorm he was used to. In fact, compared to the abuse he took from the video with his grandpa five years ago, the comments about the mask felt like cold shower droplets—not the most comfortable, but easy to dodge.

"They're really ripping apart this mask," Rick said.

"You're not gonna delete the channel, are you?"

"Nah, might delete the mask though." He went back to Shawn's channel. Someone like him probably never went through an insult storm like Rick. If he got just one bad comment, he'd probably fall apart like cheap toilet paper. He bet the words would ring in Shawn's ears forever, and *someone* had to educate him. He was probably surrounded by nothing but yes-men wanting to hug his fame in the hope some would rub off on them.

Back in the basement, Rick propped his phone up against his textbooks once more and tossed the mask aside. No matter what he did online, someone would find a way to insult him; he may as well let himself breathe. By the time he finished the warm energy had fizzled, leaving a hollowness in his gut. He'd never felt further from his skin, like his entire being clung to his bones, trying to retract from the world. The review of Shawn's album was uploaded with almost no editing and the link privatized. He changed his password so Genie wouldn't be able to sneak in and delete it or upload it.

"You sure about this?" she texted him ten minutes later.

Truthfully, he wasn't sure about it, and a small part of him wanted to delete the video on the spot. What was the best that could come from posting? Even if people agreed with him, how long would it take for them to start linking the old video all over again? He wasn't ready to welcome that back into his life, but if the girl at the corner store was any indicator, that part of his life was never going away. It would be in his obituary one day, and if he hid the rest of his life, that would be all he was remembered for. Whereas Shawn would be worshipped as some ahead-of-his-time music god because he made a few thousand people laugh when they were kids. He didn't have anyone who was a fan of his work, they just loved him, and fuck that. He had everything he wanted to the point he got bored and had to steal other people's dreams.

He wasn't sure if he was *ready* to post it, but he was sure he *wanted* to.

Chapter 9

"What is it?" Athena asked, slamming Lindsey's apartment door behind her. "You texted me '911, major emergency'." Athena had clearly just rolled out of bed, her thick black hair tied up in a messy bun on top of her head with frizzy wisps around her face. She wore boxer-style pajama shorts and a spaghetti strap tank top. Lindsey had always been jealous of how Athena could just walk around wearing next to nothing; she was so thin, she swam in whatever clothes she wore. Lindsey, even though she was fairly petite at 5'2", had boobs bigger than her head and an ass almost big enough to match. Last time she wore something as small as Athena's current outfit to run down to the lobby for coffee, Francisco had yelled at her to put some clothes on.

Regardless, Lindsey was still in her old My Chemical Romance T-shirt from high school, which she'd cut the neckline out of, and her plaid pajama pants that dragged on the floor beneath her feet.

"You might want to sit down for this," Lindsey said, picking up her laptop off the desk.

"Okay." Athena sat cross-legged on Lindsey's beat-up beige corduroy couch and folded her hands in her lap, awaiting whatever Lindsey's emergency was going to be.

"I really don't know how to tell you this, so I think I'm going to have to show you instead."

Lindsey sat down on the couch next to Athena, holding her laptop close to her chest. "You, uh… you haven't seen Shawn Boston's new album yet, have you?"

Athena rolled her eyes. "Oh my God, Lindsey. This is why you badgered me out of bed at this ungodly hour?"

"It's almost noon."

"911 texts are for *real* emergencies. Not for fangirling over Shawn's new—"

Lindsey whipped her laptop around, so the screen was facing Athena. "Shawn stole your art."

Athena stared at the screen for a moment. Her eyes went through a range of emotions, from wide and shocked, to creased and sad. "Wow," she said.

"Yeah."

"I mean, that's *definitely Grape Nipples*." Athena leaned her head in closer to the laptop screen, staring at the picture even closer.

"I can zoom in all the way if you want, but it's definitely your art," said Lindsey.

After what seemed like a full minute of awkward silence, all Athena could say was, "But… how?"

"How what?"

"How did he even get a hold of my art?"

Lindsey shrugged. "Maybe he just googled 'fruit on a naked lady' and this image came up, and he didn't give a fuck whose art he was stealing?"

Athena shook her head, letting her loose dark hair hit her in the face. "That's impossible."

"I mean, ever since I made the online store for Punk

Kitty, I've always been at least a little worried that someone might try to copy it, but I never thought—"

"But that's just it," said Athena. "I've never put this on the internet. Ever."

That's right, Lindsey remembered. Athena was always making such a big deal about how she never wanted to have an online store or social media pages or anything; Athena was the one who went the extra mile to protect herself against things like this, and here she was, the victim of theft and plagiarism.

"Well, you've sold a lot of copies of it, right?" said Lindsey. "Maybe someone who bought it was friends with Shawn and gave it to him. We've met a lot of people at the conventions we've done. Who knows what someone might've—"

"Oh no," said Athena. She pulled her knees up to her chest, resting her chin on them, a look of utter defeat taking over her eyes.

"What is it?"

"Someone does know Shawn."

"Who?"

"Elise Shiloh."

Everything suddenly clicked in Lindsey's mind. "You mean..."

"I sent her that email to enter my art in her contest. I just can't believe she would give someone else's work to Shawn like that. But Elise would never do that! Right? Maybe Shawn stole it from her..." Athena trailed off, her face now expressionless from the shock.

"Regardless of who's at fault, someone stole your art, Athena. You need to get justice."

"Justice?"

"Yeah! Shawn's going to sell millions of copies of this.

You could be getting paid for that. You could sue him. Or Elise."

"We don't have any real proof though."

"Real proof? Athena, your art is there on the screen! You emailed it to Elise. You have that email. There's ample proof on Elise's blog and on Shawn's channel that they know each other."

"That's not enough proof for court," Athena said, shaking her head. "My grandma's a lawyer. I've seen enough of how this plays out. Shawn and Elise would both hire lawyers that make even more than my rich grandma does. They would both find a million loopholes and ways to discredit me. Plus, since I've never put this art on the internet, there aren't public time stamps to show that I made this before the album came out. We could probably get testimony from a few people who have bought it in the past, but I've never stayed in contact with any of them. I'd end up spending the rest of the rent money my grandma gave me on legal fees."

"What if you hired your grandma to defend you in court?"

Athena shook her head even harder, her chin still resting on top of her knees. "Grandma is a personal injury and workers' compensation lawyer. She's never practiced intellectual property law. And she almost always works on out-of-court settlements. She rarely goes to trial."

Lindsey hadn't realized there was a difference between types of lawyers. After the number of times, she'd watched the movie *My Cousin Vinny*, she'd kind of assumed lawyers just all did the same kind of lawyer stuff and floated between different lawyer categories as they were needed.

"Well, there's got to be something we can do," said Lindsey.

Athena shrugged. "We can eat double our weight in ice

cream and cry for a few days, then get back to working on our art."

That's just like Athena, Lindsey thought, *to give up so easily.* Athena was used to being passive, which Lindsey had noticed with her non-assertive style of salesmanship.

But that made sense, that Athena didn't know how to make a sales pitch even after taking Elise Shiloh's course— Elise was kind of a fraud after all, right? Lindsey thought back to the DrawmaLlamas video she'd watched last night, which exposed Elise as a "scammer supreme."

That video, which had hundreds of thousands of views. That video, which exposed Elise for who she was.

"I know what we can do," Lindsey said.

An hour later, Athena was nervously pacing around Lindsey's kitchen while Lindsey stood hunched over her desk, connecting her drawing tablet to her laptop.

"I don't know about this," Athena fretted.

"Just send me the screenshot. I need 'receipts.' I think that's what the DrawmaLlamas called it last night. I need proof of what we're talking about to show the audience. Trust me, YouTube channels like the DrawmaLlamas do this all the time."

"I really don't want to get involved in internet drama."

"I think calling this internet drama is a little reductive, don't you?" Lindsey protested. "This isn't some makeup community infighting or something stupid like that. This is art theft."

Athena wove her fingers through her hair, pulling more of it loose from the bun. She continued to move back and forth on the cool tile floor of the kitchen, barefoot, taking three steps in each direction before turning around and backtracking. "I don't know. There's a reason I don't put myself out there online."

"Yeah, and what is that reason, exactly? You've still never clarified—"

"Don't worry about it!" Athena snapped. She closed her eyes and took a moment to calm down, taking a deep breath and exhaling slowly. "I'm sorry. What I mean is, I don't want to be involved in any of this. I've seen how brutal the online world can be. I just want to sell my art to people who want to buy it. I don't want to deal with these conflicts where we all, I don't know, *cancel* each other or whatever."

Lindsey shook her head. "I'm not trying to 'cancel' Shawn or Elise. I just want to make it clear that the art they're using is stolen."

"But what if we're wrong? What if Elise didn't really send Shawn that picture? My grandma's dealt with false accusations before. People get really upset about slander. We can't afford a slander suit..."

Lindsey sat down in her desk chair and thought for a moment. "Okay, fair enough. So, we don't bring Elise into this at all. We know for a fact that this is your art, and that Shawn is using it on an album he's selling. That's all we know for sure, but it's enough."

"I'm sorry, Lindsey," Athena said. "I know that you want to help me, and I appreciate that, but I just can't. This all makes me too nervous. I'm just... I'm just gonna go back to bed for now and figure it out later."

"It's almost two in the afternoon."

"Yeah, and it's another Saturday without a convention. We have enough to worry about right now without trying to take down someone huge like Shawn Boston."

"We don't need to take him down, we just—"

"I'm going back to bed." Athena headed back toward

the apartment door. "I'll be upstairs asleep for the next couple hours. Maybe you should get some extra rest too. You're clearly hung over and I don't want you to do something we'll both regret."

Lindsey sat in her desk chair staring at the door Athena had just closed. As much as she hated to admit it, this wasn't just about Athena. Lindsey had chosen to put her art online, and if someone as low-key and offline as Athena could get her art stolen by someone huge, then Lindsey's work was at risk too. As an artist, she couldn't let a thief like Shawn Boston get away with this.

At the same time, Lindsey felt conflicted. Over the past month, she'd become a huge fan of Shawn. His videos had inspired her. He made her believe that, even in a worldwide pandemic that shut down every in-person event, she could still make a living as an artist. He had inspired her to start her own channel in the first place.

She knew that if she made this video, it was likely a LOT of people would see it. The DrawmaLlamas were proof of that; conflict sold online.

Lindsey opened up her screen recording software, started Photoshop, turned on the laptop's microphone, and hit record.

"Hey, it's Lindsey, creator of Punk Kitty," she said. "And today I have some sad news. Shawn Boston stole my best friend's art."

Lindsey recorded for about an hour. Taking a page out of the DrawmaLlamas' book, she drew a picture of Shawn while she talked about the situation and how it transpired. Then, when it was time to edit the video, she went onto her cloud drive and downloaded some photos she had of her and Athena at recent conventions. Any photo where *Grape Nipples* was visible got added to the video. Out of respect for her friend, Lindsey blurred Athena's face in every image. But she made sure to zoom in on the painting. Then, she added the pictures of Shawn's new album.

"These are the pictures of my friend at a few different art conventions with me," she said on the voice recording. "And you know these were all months ago. We're in a pandemic right now, and none of these events are happening anymore. She first created this piece over a year ago and has been selling it everywhere since."

When Lindsey was done editing, she waited for the video to export, gently swiveling herself back and forth in her chair. This had major potential to make Athena mad. But then again, Athena pretty much never went on YouTube, so how would she even find out it existed? Lindsey never mentioned Athena's name. She did every-thing possible to protect her identity. The truth was, Shawn needed to be called out for this.

By the time the sun was setting outside her window that Saturday evening, Lindsey had uploaded the video file to her YouTube channel. She looked at her sad little chan-nel, with two subscribers (a guy named "sendMeYourTid-desPlz" and the girl who had commented "cute kitty" on the first video) and only 14 views. As much as she hated to admit it, she knew this video had the potential to help her channel. She was going to be the first person to call Shawn Boston out publicly online, just like the DrawmaLlamas were for Elise Shiloh. *But that's not why I'm doing this,* Lindsey told herself. *Even if that would be a really nice bonus...*

She hit "publish" and let out a heavy sigh.

Then, she grabbed a bottle of wine from her kitchen nook; her last one. She opened it up and tipped it toward her mouth, drinking the stress away.

Lindsey made a point not to look at her YouTube page at all for the rest of the night. She just couldn't. She was certain Athena was up from her nap by now, but she hadn't received any angry texts, so she knew Athena hadn't seen the video. And how would she? Athena wasn't one of her two subscribers. Athena never went on social media at all.

By midnight, Lindsey was too drunk to resist temptation anymore. She plopped down in her desk chair, and she opened her laptop back up. Then she refreshed her YouTube page.

She knew it was going to be good, but she didn't expect it to be *this* good.

In the 6 hours since she'd posted her video, it was already up to 50,000 views. She'd gained over 10,000 subscribers. And the comment section was full of people expressing various versions of the same sentiment:

"Shawn Boston is CANCELED!"

Chapter 10

B efore he went to bed, the primary searches sending
people to Rick's channel were two punk bands, a rap
artist, and loads of furry community videos. But when
Genie woke him up with a "You gotta see this," that all
changed. Shawn Boston Hater, Shawn Boston Sucks, and
a dozen other anti-Shawn-Boston channels dominated his
algorithm, and his subscriber count broke 1,000
overnight.

At least the furry comments stopped, though people
were talking shit about his musical abilities and song selec-
tion: "Who is he to say anyone sucks?" a pictureless avatar
asked under his most recent drumming video.

"You're blowing up, dude," Genie said.

She wasn't kidding. For the first time, Rick had thousands of views on his video, and the "recommended" tab
showed that his wasn't the only one. Some gorgeous girl
named PunkKitty tore Shawn apart and—"Holy shit this is
taking off," he said, more about PunkKitty's video than his,
but Genie agreed.

"And look at all the people agreeing with you."

"Nah, check this out," he sent her a link to PunkKitty's video.

"Cute. Busty."

"Very."

"Looks painful." Genie spoke like she was studying an art history textbook.

"Looks nice to me," Rick grinned.

"No shit. Those definitely help with her views too," Genie sneered. Sensing Rick was about to say something, she added, "What? It's true."

"She gets it, though," Rick said as he listened to her pick Shawn apart. The album art was the one thing he liked about the project. "Of course, he stole it. Guys like him can get away with anything and his fans will always defend him."

"Whoa, she's ripping him a new one," Genie replied.

"I gotta talk to her." Rick initially typed out a short supportive message, but two words of encouragement turned into a sentence. "I wouldn't be surprised if he's ripping off more people too," he typed out, which led to a paragraph defending the point. "And I have to bring up how bad the music is too, right?" he asked Genie, but didn't pay attention to her answer; he was already bashing the over-polished turd who tried to convince the world he was a gemstone.

"Look at her subs!" Genie said but Rick wasn't paying attention.

"She's amazing," he heard the dreaminess in his own voice and straightened his face as if that could retroactively yank the words from the air and erase the goofy grin, he rocked just a moment ago. Suddenly feeling nervous, Rick wondered whether he could actually press "send" on the comment. His finger hovered over the "backspace" button.

"Careful, don't go falling in love on the internet again,"

Genie joked, and Rick smiled sheepishly. It wasn't his favorite memory, and she was kind enough not to hold it over his head too often since he was usually having a bad enough day already.

"Thought you promised to let that go."

"How could I ever let that go? *You loved me!*" She emphasized the last three words like Bugs Bunny and made a fake kissing sound.

"By never bringing it up again."

"Where's the fun in that? Besides if you start blowing up, you'll need someone to keep you in your place," Genie chuckled.

"I think I've had more than enough of that in my lifetime." He didn't need Genie reminding him of those feelings she had struck down on the spot as swiftly as a mosquito by the lake.

"Maybe if you get famous enough you can ask her out."

"Yeah, maybe I should wait until I'm famous enough." With that, Rick started smashing the backspace button on his comment.

"Wait, you're wimping out already? Rick, I was just kidding!"

Rick stopped listening to Genie the second he saw a red notification by his name. "Dude, *she* commented on *my* video." He read the message out loud to Genie who didn't say much. In fact, Rick couldn't remember the last time she was left completely speechless. "You there?"

"Yeah, just getting distracted by the cat. I think I gotta go." She hung up before he could say goodbye. That was the sort of move he would do, and Rick wondered what he had done wrong. If anyone had the right to be annoyed from the conversation it was him. Genie was the one bringing up yet another embarrassing moment from his past to "keep him humble." Like he needed any extra help with that. He went back to his video, reading over the comment again. Here he was thinking she would be terrified by the psycho stranger who blasted her comment section with a manifesto, but she not only liked it, she hit him right back with one of her own. He pinned the comment and left his room, seeing no sign of his grandpa. The whole city seemed to be shutting down, so Rick had no idea where he could be running off to all this time.

Like a fishing pole, the vibrating phone in his pocket kept reeling him back to YouTube. PunkKitty shared his video, and his subs were growing by the minute. As much as he wanted to celebrate, the empty apartment was a cold reminder that his grandfather was probably out working, risking his health, to afford this place while Rick sat online. He still hadn't heard from Rufus about what was happening at the club, but the week was coming to a close and he had no idea if he should show up for his next shift.

He tried calling Rufus, and his fears were confirmed when it went right to voicemail. As he went down to the basement his phone buzzed again, only this time it wasn't the percussion of subscriber notifications that yanked Rick's attention away.

He had rarely spoken to Penny at work, and forgot he even had her name in his phone but the text that flashed across the screen was enough to send Rick's soul from his body like vibrations off a kick drum: "Rufus tested positive. Everyone who was at work last week has to quarantine."

"Are you kidding me?" Rick texted back.

"Who is this?"

Rick's mouth twitched. Of course, it was a mass group text. He couldn't tell if he wanted to laugh or melt into a puddle. There was no middle ground for him; people either knew him as a meme or didn't know he existed.

"Yes, all Low Octave staff who worked our last night must quarantine for two weeks."

Rick's pulse quickened. Self-quarantine? Lock himself in his room for two weeks? What about his grandpa? Was he already exposed? Should he tell him to stay or leave? He felt dizzy and leaned against the sofa. His face felt numb, and he slid to the floor.

What if he had it? Would this really be his life? The moment he put something online that didn't turn him into a meme was the moment he died from a plague? He'd be one of those legendary clowns who had the decency to die young before becoming a serial killer. He was that unlucky kid who just got his life in order and gave a huge fist pump, only to immediately get struck down by lightning.

"Can we talk?" he messaged Genie, but even she wasn't getting back to him now. He was feeling on top of the world just five minutes ago; how did he find a rock to trip over so quickly?

The front door opened, and he covered his face like a vampire watching the sunrise. "Stay back!" he said. He heard a pair of keys fall into a ceramic bowl.

"What drugs are you on?" his grandpa's nasally voice broke the silence. Rick half expected the world to fall apart around him like a kid's shitty block tower.

"Rufus got it. I probably have it," Rick replied, and silence seeped back into the room. At first it felt like a hesitation, and he expected his grandpa to say something—anything. He could've taken it in one of two directions: the comforting father figure, or the furious high-risk individual. Both men settling for silence simultaneously shifted the weight back and forth over the room like an elephant on a circus ball—fitting for a clown to balance his life on one. Even the slightest wavering sent his whole world rocking.

"How do you feel?" his grandpa finally asked.

"Not bad, I mean—I don't know." Rick put the back of his hand to his forehead. "Hot."

"Hot like *hot* hot, or like you're freaking out hot?"

"I don't know."

"Well, are you freaking out?"

"Of course, I'm freaking out!" Rick's voice rose.

"How were you feeling before the news?"

"What?"

"Before the news." He crossed the room and crouched in front of Rick whose first reaction was to cover his face with his hands. "Before you found out, were you feeling sick?"

Rick shook his head. Before he found out he felt ready to run six marathons backwards. His grandpa sighed and rubbed the top of his head like it was a combo magic 8 ball and golden retriever. "It's all in your head."

"What? No, I got the text, I was exposed."

"Of course, you were, and you might have it, but whatever you're feeling right now isn't it." He walked to the sink and filled a glass with water.

"What're you doing? You can't stay here. If I, have it and you get sick you could—"

"Die? Yeah, but leaving now won't change the fact that we've been living together this past week." He pulled the half-eaten pint of ice cream from the freezer and grabbed a spoon out of the drawer. "The worst thing we could do right now is panic."

"Grandpa?" Rick followed him to the couch.

"I know you, okay? I know your mind jumps to worst case scenarios before the sentence is even finished. If you won the lottery, you'd be freaking out about who was gonna rob you. Obviously, me," he pointed the spoon to his chest.

Rick kept his mouth closed because he wanted to

believe the things his grandpa was saying, but he felt like he walked through a cobweb. He couldn't just shake COVID off and if he was exposed—he pulled his shirt over his mouth.

"Now what're you doing?" his grandpa asked.

Rick took two large steps back until his butt hit the kitchen table. "I don't want to get you sick."

"You look like a jackass. I already said we would've both been exposed to it by now if you were, so the best thing to do is stay calm. That means don't go full ninja with a t-shirt over your face when you're inside your own home. I'll think you're trying to rob me."

Rick leaned back against the table until his grandpa snapped his fingers. "And how many times do I gotta tell ya, keep your ass off surfaces we eat off of."

"What're we gonna do?"

"Well, I'm gonna tell Sven that by no fault of our own we don't have the money this month, and hopefully get an extension." His grandpa reached for the remote and began flipping through channels.

"And me?"

"Just don't talk to anyone if you think you got it, and maybe don't go down to your drums until the hall is empty," he added. Rick hadn't even thought about not having access to his drums. What if it was a whole week before he could get back down there safely? His thoughts began to spiral when his grandpa interrupted them.

"Oh, and keep looking for a job."

The words thumped against his stomach as he turned to head back to his room. Still, it could've been worse. His heart rate slowed, and he took a deep breath. Well, at least he could still do that. He wasn't burning up and didn't have a cough. Maybe he would be fine.

When he got back to his computer, he saw a new notification on YouTube and gasped: PunkKitty had commented on his video! Reading over her message, he realized her problem with Shawn was more than a disliking of his content and brand. She had something personal against him, and the more he read the more it fueled his disdain for the influencer. Even the term made his skin crawl. *Influencer*. Influencing what? Shitty taste in music. He was no longer just the image obsessed, autotuned, online personality. He was a liar and a thief who needed a wakeup call. He replied to the comment, still unable to believe the gorgeous girl with thousands of subs reached out to him of all people—and not to laugh at him over some viral video from five years ago, but for something he created.

He hit send before he could add anything that made him sound like an idiot, and leaned back in his chair. Shawn Boston was going down.

Chapter 11

L indsey couldn't sleep.

Every time she lay in her bed, arms flopped behind her head, trying to keep her eyes shut, she'd end up feeling restless. First, her legs would twitch a little, then she'd try to shift to a new position. Maybe roll around to her front. Nope, sleeping on your front with boobs that size was a recipe for waking up feeling like an airbag had hit you.

Plus, her mind couldn't rest. No matter how many times she tried to flip over in bed, or slightly change the position of head on the pillow, all she could see in her mind were those 50,000 views on her video, and all those comments about Shawn Boston being canceled.

Part of her felt guilty, as much as she hated to admit it.

The guilt was a weird mixture of pride and remorse. Pride over her instant 50,000 views and her thousands of new viewers and subscribers—pride over finally being noticed on the vast sea of the internet. But then came the guilt; as much as she wanted to deny it, part of the guilt was over the pride she felt. Why did she feel good about gaining so much attention at the expense of someone else?

That was another part of the guilt. Sure, she thought her video might get some traction—after all, that's how the DrawmaLlamas made their whole career. She never expected it to blow up *this* quickly, though. What if this actually ruined Shawn's life?

Then again, Shawn had been the one to steal Athena's art. Didn't he deserve it?

Lindsey couldn't fucking sleep.

So, she hauled her only-slightly-sobered-up ass out of bed at 2 in the morning, sat back down in her desk chair, and immersed herself in the world of internet drama once again.

"Shawn Boston is CANCELED."

"I always knew something wasn't right with Shawn."

"Looking back, this actually makes sense. Shawn always made the most unoriginal music ever. Of course, he steals art, too."

"I can't believe I was a fan of Shawn for so long! I hope you guys can forgive me."

"Ew I always knew Shawn was gross. Why didn't anyone listen to me when I tried to tell them on Twitter?"

"Who is the artist he stole from? Can we buy THAT PERSON'S stuff instead?"

"I wish I could get a refund for the album I preordered, now that I know Shawn STOLE THE ART!"

"Do you guys think Shawn's MUSIC is even original either?"

"I stand with the artist! I do NOT stand with Shawn!"

"Shawn is SO CANCELED."

. . .

The comments hurt Lindsey's head. Just a day ago, there were almost no criticisms of Shawn on the entire internet. Almost everything she could find when she searched for him was praise. Now that she'd posted a video exposing him, a ton of fans were coming out of the woodwork to act like they'd hated Shawn all along.

Or did they hate him all along and didn't want to speak up?

Lindsey continued to scroll.

Around 3:30 that morning, she'd finished reading through and responding to every comment on the video. Taking a deep breath and flopping back in her chair Lindsey finally felt ready to go to bed. She was about to close out of her video, when—

Lindsey noticed the list of recommended videos along the side of her screen. There was another one like hers that had just been posted yesterday by some guy named BigRickEnergy.

"All These Things that Shawn Has Done."

She couldn't help herself. Her eyes were so tired they felt like they were on fire. Her face hurt from how hard she had to force them open. But her mind was whirling at a mile a minute; no matter how badly her eyes begged for sleep, her mind refused. She clicked on the thumbnail.

In the video was a slightly chubby guy sitting at a drum set. She sat there and watched, mesmerized, as he played a cover of the Killers' "All These Things That I've Done" but with lyrics detailing all the reasons he found Shawn Boston to be fake. Why he found him to be an insult to what serious musicians desperately want—and often struggle—to achieve in their careers.

Apparently, his video was blowing up, too.

As she listened, she left him a comment: "I'm glad I'm not the only one."

By the time BigRickEnergy's half-hour-long video on Shawn was over, Lindsey realized she had so much more to say. "I'm glad I'm not the only one" wasn't going to cut it; not when the two of them seemed to be the only people on the internet brave enough to take on Shawn Boston.

She began writing a second comment.

"Shawn Boston stole my best friend's art," she wrote. "I'm not sure if you've seen my video on it. I just posted it —around the same time you did, oddly enough. I never wanted to be one of those people who goes into other people's comment sections to promote their own videos, but I'm just saying that to let you know I'm on your side here. I have to admit, when I first posted the video, I felt kind of guilty. Weird, right? I was actually a fan of Shawn for a while. His music was kind of getting me through the pandemic these past couple weeks. But now I feel bad about that, now that you've really correctly pointed out what was so wrong with his music. You're right that Shawn doesn't care about musical integrity; he just wants to be an influencer. So, all I'm trying to say is, thanks for this video. Hit me up if you ever want to collab sometime."

That was a new term Lindsey had recently learned from watching so many YouTube videos over the past two months: "collab." Short for "collaborate." Sometimes the DrawmaLlamas collabed with other art channels or other drama channels, and it always accelerated their views since the videos got views from both parties' core audiences. Maybe she and this BigRickEnergy guy could do that too.

With her comment sent, Lindsey was finally ready to head to bed. She grabbed her phone off her desk and walked the couple feet back over to her bed. She set her phone down on the nightstand, dropped her pants, whipped off her shirt, and slid under the covers naked.

Then, before she could fall asleep, her phone started vibrating against the nightstand.

She tried to ignore it, but it vibrated a second time. Then a third.

Finally, she rolled over once again to see her phone screen lighting up.

An email notification. From the Punk Kitty store.

Lindsey had sold 50 enamel pins in the past hour.

Her eyes, which had been fighting not to close just moments ago, sprung open like a jack-in-the-box. She stared at the screen wide-eyed. 50 enamel pins in one hour.

Those were... those were *convention* numbers. Those were CreateCon numbers.

She flung her blanket off and, without putting her clothes back on, hopped back into her desk chair. She opened her laptop back up and logged into her e-shop interface.

A few of her new orders included messages, like: "Thank you so much for finally exposing Shawn Boston for the creep he is!"

Well, Lindsey had never said he was a creep... but when that person had just bought three enamel pins, two patches, and a sheet of ten stickers, who was she to argue?

"OMG Lindsey! I found you on your Punk Kitty YouTube channel from your video about Shawn Boston!! I'm so glad you finally said what we were all thinking! Then I saw your cat drawing video and I realized I had to support you!"

I said what we were all thinking. Lindsey wondered. She didn't even realize that hating Shawn was on everyone's mind.

"Your channel has SERIOUS DrawmaLlama energy! I was looking for another channel like them to follow! So glad I found you! Love to support artists like you & the

Drawma fam. I bought one of your prints along with the enamel pins—can you sign it for me?"

In the span of a few hours, Lindsey had gone from a broke nobody selling nothing... to a full-on E-Thot McGee.

A new order came in a moment later with an even longer message: "Lindsey, I am so grateful I found you. I saw you linked your store in your video description, so I was happy to buy some of your art. I thought your video on Shawn was so thoughtful and it really emphasized how someone who thinks he's larger than life can hurt people on an individual level, like how he stole your friend's art. I commend you for having the courage to speak out against someone so huge with so much influence. I really hope you'll make more videos on Shawn. There aren't a lot of people out there who are willing to call out bigger creators like him. Just you and one other guy I saw, Big Rick or something? Anyway, I want to see more of you. Thanks for doing what you do."

The strange mixed feeling of pride and remorse began rearing its ugly, nauseating head once again. What was this? What was the tightness in her stomach and the thumping of her heart trying to tell her? Why did her head feel hot, and her fingers feel tingly all at once?

Excitement coursed through her body; after months with limited human contact, Lindsey suddenly had a wave of attention crashing into her. After months of little to no income, she had orders flooding her inbox. After weeks barely hitting double digits on her YouTube channel, she suddenly had a real fan base.

She stared at the comment on the screen in front of her. "I hope you'll make more videos on Shawn... I want to see more of you."

This was what people wanted from her now: videos

about Shawn. But how was she going to continue this? What else could she even say to criticize Shawn again?

Lindsey had been a fan of Shawn up until he stole Athena's art; and really, that was the only negative thing she knew about him, other than what she'd just learned from BigRickEnergy's video.

BigRickEnergy's video. That was it.

She pulled his video up again, scrolling through the comments to see if he'd answered hers yet. He hadn't. But he also hadn't answered any comments left in the past seven hours. Judging by the way he talked, Lindsey assumed he was American, so it was likely the middle of the night for him too.

Then she saw his video description: "Email me here if you want to talk or maybe book me to play drums at your show or something."

A potential YouTube video collab probably counted as "wanting to talk," or maybe even "or something." She wrote a quick email to BigRickEnergy introducing herself, then watched his video again.

He was cute.

His voice was cute, too, in its own weird way. She detected a slight accent, maybe New York? Something East Coast for sure. It was cute how he sounded nervous when he talked. It was cute how he fiddled with his drumsticks. He seemed kind of shy, but he was out here in front of thousands of people kicking Shawn Boston's proverbial ass. And something about that was cute as hell, too.

At ten o'clock that morning, Lindsey realized she'd fallen asleep naked in her desk chair. Just another Sunday.

She awoke half slouched over with her legs spilling over the side of her spinny desk chair. Her neck, craned to the side, hurt like hell. The weight of her entire head almost rested on her own left shoulder. She stretched her arms wide, letting the muscles in her shoulders roll back into place, then slowly cracked her neck, cringing at the soreness as she turned it.

Since she'd fallen asleep in front of the computer without realizing it, her laptop was still open to her YouTube page, where she had over 200 new notifications. She checked them: a new video comment here, a new message there. Then, she saw a reply from BigRickEnergy: "Nice to meet you. I liked your video too."

Lindsey began typing a reply. "Want to collab sometime?"

A minute later, he had replied again.

BigRickEnergy: Maybe. I've never done a collab before though.

PunkKitty: Me either. My channel is super new. But I figured, hey, we both got beef with Shawn Boston, huh? So, might as well make more videos & give the people what they want!

BigRickEnergy: The people really do want it, don't they? I don't know what your channel was like before, but mine blew up overnight.

PunkKitty: Same! I had like 2 subscribers, and now I have—

. . .

Lindsey stopped typing for a moment to check her subscriber count; it had increased to 20,000 just since she and BigRickEnergy had begun talking

PunkKitty: like 20,000?! That's amazing!

BigRickEnergy: woah! That's a ton.

PunkKitty: I guess people kind of hated Shawn all along?

BigRickEnergy: Yeah. I was surprised. I was really nervous I was going to get hate for this video.

Lindsey hadn't even thought of that. The idea of random people online hating her had somehow never crossed her mind; mass online hatred seemed like things that only happened to bigger e-celebrities, like E-Thot McGee and Elise Shiloh and, now, Shawn Boston. The only fear Lindsey had about posting the video—which unfortunately was still living rent-free inside her stomach—was that Athena would be super mad if she found out. Even though Lindsey didn't show Athena's name or face, and even though she made the video to defend her. But Athena didn't use the internet much, so she probably wouldn't find out, right?

PunkKitty: I'm glad you didn't get any hate. Want to plan a collab?

. . .

BigRickEnergy: I guess we could... people would probably want to see that, wouldn't they?

PunkKitty: Definitely. Email me. punkkittybylindsey-drake@coolmail.mail

When Lindsey closed her laptop, she wasn't sure if she'd hear back from BigRickEnergy. He didn't seem too hyped on the idea of a collab, even if they both knew it would get the views.

Still exhausted, Lindsey decided to head down to the lobby for some fancy Keurig machine coffee. As she made herself presentable (clothes, slippers, face mask) and headed toward the elevator, she silently prayed she wouldn't run into Francisco along the way.

Thankfully, she didn't. Unfortunately, however, today's trip to the coffee maker wasn't totally drama-free.

No sooner had Lindsey hit the glowing "Brew 8 oz." button on the Keurig than she was the target of yet another verbal assault at the coffee maker.

"I can't believe you!"

Lindsey turned away from the steamy coffee pouring into her paper cup to face Athena, standing across from her in the mailroom.

"What?"

"I told you not to start shit online!"

This felt like one of those moments in a movie where the characters have a classic misunderstanding due to a lack of communication. Often in those movies, one character would say something like, "*But I didn't even think you used* YouTube! *How could you have possibly seen my video?!*" And then the other character would go, "*No, I was talking about something totally unrelated that I was mad at you for. Wait, you posted a video about me on* YouTube? *Now I'm mad at you for* TWO THINGS!*"*

Lindsey wasn't going to let herself fall into that trap. So instead, she said, "What shit online?"

Athena rolled her eyes, crossing her arms. "Does a video titled 'Shawn Boston Stole My Best Friend's Art' ring a bell?"

Fuck. So, Lindsey's plan to pretend she had no idea what was going on was a complete failure. "Yeah," was all she could think to say.

"I told you not to make a video about me! And you did it anyway! Why?"

"Uh, to defend you?"

"But is it even really defending me if I literally told you not to do it?"

"But I didn't really make a video about YOU," Lindsey argued. "I made a video about Shawn. I didn't even mention your name. I blocked out your name everywhere. I blocked out your face in the pictures I showed of us at the conventions. No one would even know it was YOU."

"Yeah, except all my fans who recognize *Grape Nipples!*"

"Those fans would *already* recognize it as Shawn's album cover!"

Athena paused, looking taken aback for a moment. "Wait, I guess you're right."

"How did you even come across the video anyway? I thought you didn't use social media for anything."

"I don't!" Athena said quickly—too quickly, Lindsey thought. So quickly it seemed suspicious, though Lindsey couldn't quite point out why.

"Then how did you find the video?"

"Because," she said, pausing, unfolding her arms, and moving her hands down to her hips. Still a sassy pose, but slightly less threatening, Lindsey thought. "Because," Athena continued, "I thought you might do something like this. After I left your apartment yesterday, you seemed like you weren't fully convinced that you shouldn't do this. So, I kind of suspected you might post something anyway."

"Athena, I didn't want the video to upset you."

"Yeah," she rolled her eyes again. "You just hoped I wouldn't see it."

"I don't get why you're mad at me. You should be mad at Shawn for stealing your art."

Athena dropped her arms to her sides; all pretenses of aggression were gone. "I *am* mad at Shawn. That's the thing! I'm so, so goddamn fucking mad at him! I don't want to be a part of any online drama, but I also have no choice! Because Shawn went and took my art and started profiting off of it like it was his own. And now I can either let it go and just suffer the payment I never got, or I can fight back and become the next E-Thot McGee. There's no middle ground, and that's so unfair to me!"

Lindsey picked up her coffee from the counter and took a long, deep sip, letting the steam rising from the cup warm her face. "I'm sorry this happened to you, Athena," she said. "It wasn't fair of Shawn to do that. And I'm sorry you found out about the video like this. I just didn't know what else to do. I couldn't let him get away with it."

"Well, how has the response been so far?" Athena asked.

"Oh my god, it's been *amazing!*" said Lindsey. "Everyone is pissed at Shawn."

"Yeah?" Athena murmured, walking toward Lindsey.

Side by side, they headed over to the elevator, which

they entered together. "Yeah. I don't know if you read any of the comments."

"I couldn't bring myself too. I actually couldn't even finish the video. I was just... so scared, you know?"

"I know," said Lindsey. With her paper cup of coffee in one hand, she reached her other hand toward the elevator buttons.

"Let's go to my apartment," Athena said. "Yours is too full of internet drama. Mine is full of art. I need to work on some new pieces anyway."

Lindsey pressed the "7", Athena's floor, and they rode the slow, rickety elevator up together.

"I know you don't want to keep talking about the video," Lindsey said. "But I got a few comments from people saying they supported you." She paused for a moment when she saw Athena's forehead beginning to crinkle in concern. "Not you as in *you*. They still don't know who you are. I mean, they said they support the artist. Some people said they wished they knew who you were so they could buy your stuff."

Athena sighed. "I wish they could."

Lindsey wasn't going to push the online store issue, not right now—not when Athena had just been dealt this blow. Instead, they waited for the elevator to ding on floor 7, and then headed out to Athena's apartment together.

"You know, some guy posted a video the same day as me criticizing Shawn," Lindsey noted as they walked down the long, gray-carpeted hallway to Athena's unit. "Some guy named BigRickEnergy. He's kinda cute."

Athena rolled her eyes once again, this time punctuating it with a small laugh. "Are you two gonna—oh, what's it called?—*collab* or something?"

"I don't know. I'm still not sure if he wants to."

Athena slid her key into her apartment's front door,

then flung it open. She and Lindsey entered Chez Athena, a tiny studio apartment filled with stretched canvases on easels, watercolor paintings thumbtacked all over the walls, jars of every type of paint—oil, acrylic, watercolor, tempera, you name it—on the coffee table, and unfinished pieces of art all over the couch, the kitchen, and Athena's folding card table-slash-desk. Additionally, Athena's floor was littered with half-eaten takeout boxes from Chinese restaurants, Thai restaurants, Italian restaurants, and more. Lindsey had always been grateful to have a friend who was physically much messier than she was; that said a lot.

Athena moved an oil painting to the side so Lindsey could sit on the couch. Lindsey sat down, careful that her feet didn't knock over the jar of acrylic paint on the floor right next to her.

Athena then picked up one of her half-finished pieces and brought her canvas over to one of the easels. "I'm going to work on this while we talk if you don't mind."

Lindsey nodded. Then, she felt her phone buzz in her pocket.

Sliding the phone out, Lindsey checked the notifications. First, an email notification for a new set of enamel pin and patch orders. Then, an email from Rick.

Chapter 12

O nce Rick finally worked up the courage to actually
email PunkKitty, the idea of a collab started to
sound better and better. After he sent the first email, he
was surprised at how quickly she replied, girls usually
didn't reply to him within the first hour, if at all. But Punk-
Kitty, whose name he'd learned was Lindsey, was bursting
with collab ideas.

They sent scripts back and forth to one another, asking
for input on the videos where their own knowledge was
light. Of course, this meant Rick was the one dragging
Lindsey down most of the time. She was the one with all
the information on Shawn and the first-hand experience of
someone getting screwed over by him. All Rick had was
taste.

"I'll never respect someone who steals from artists," he
told Lindsey. It was far from the first time he said it, but
having someone as pretty as her *talking* to him—and not
just laughing—still felt too good to be true. He had
resigned himself to feeling content in silence this past year,
making it through an evening at Low Octave without a

single photo, but this partnership felt real. It gave him hope that maybe he could still have some control over the way the world saw him.

A red number popped up in his inbox: another rejection. Apparently, the world wouldn't see him as employed. He wasn't optimistic about finding a job. Even when the world wasn't coming to an end no one looked at his business degree as anything more than a piece of paper with some fancy writing on it.

Genie called him the second he texted her about his latest rejection. Her voice rose. "Why are you bothering to look for work right now when you have a real chance of growing a channel?"

"Oh yeah, I'm sure my grandpa would love that. He thought getting a music degree was a waste of time, imagine explaining YouTube to him," Rick replied.

"Yeah, but you're trapped in your house right now. Plus, why would he need to know about it anyway? Once you start making money he won't care."

"I don't know if it's about the money with him," Rick said. A business degree was a suit and tie degree, the most traditional and plain resume builder. Pretty much the opposite of the video that introduced him to the world. Maybe it was an overcorrection for what he went through. Like a 401k could 401-kill the memories of sprinting by the quad every weekday his freshman year as classmates took his picture.

"Well, if you ask me, I think he owes it to you to at least let you fix your online reputation however you want. Speaking of which, how're the videos coming with Lindsey?"

Rick hopped on his bed and covered his stomach with a pillow. If only pressing one against his gut could shrink it. He couldn't ignore the fact that since he started recording without the wolf mask, the crease of his double chin smiled at the camera, excited to soak up all the attention. "Good, I think—she's like super..." he couldn't think of the right word. Intense? Thorough? Hot? "A bit of a workaholic."

"Good, you could use one of those in your life."

"One of what?"

"Someone with direction, dude."

He knew she was right, but she didn't have to say it. He had his grandpa breathing down his neck about getting a job, and now he was worried about letting Lindsey down; the last thing he needed was more stress. Letting Genie stew in the silence, he checked his email again. Two more messages from Lindsey in the last few minutes alone. "Hey one more thing, I found this article on people he's collabed with in the past. Funny, if they aren't still in his inner circle, they've pretty much disappeared."

He had nothing to add to it. Lindsey sounded like she was almost done with her next video and Rick just wanted to drum. He tapped his foot on the floor trying to keep a beat as he went back to his YouTube page. All his videos were picking up views, and new subscribers were coming in by the minute, but all their comments said the same thing:

MORE SHAWN BOSTON VIDEOS!

He hated to admit he missed the furry comments. At least they were music fans. Even if they didn't like his work, he felt like he could talk to them about something besides Shawn Boston. That was all anyone wanted to talk about. Either they hated him and cheered on his and Lindsey's videos, or they loved him and wanted Rick to play hopscotch on the thruway. He couldn't stand the guy, which made the idea of focusing his content on Shawn all the more revolting. Each time someone called him a hater, all he saw was another line connecting him to Shawn.

Even worse, the comments on his original video were filling up with URLs to *the* video and comments saying, "This you?"

Genie cleared her throat and Rick picked the phone up. "I hate it when you give me the silent treatment!"

"Got another message from Lindsey, sorry." He turned his camera on and put on his best puppy eyes, and was met by a throaty laugh.

"You gotta record something for her already." She turned on her camera too and it was enough to make Rick pause. She was sitting beside a lava lamp, wearing a onesie and giant headphones.

"You look comfortable."

"You were trying to look cute, thought I'd show you what cute really is."

The links to his old video kept pouring in. Some of them were among the top comments and had a thousand likes. Could it mean a thousand people were watching his grandpa flip him onto the pavement? He was so sure he wanted to take down Shawn Boston a few days ago, but as it refocused the attention on his past he wondered if it was worth it. He debated deleting his channel before it got any bigger—but that would mean no more Lindsey.

"Dude, you look lost."

"Sorry, just skimming the comments."

"How many times do I have to tell you, stay out of the comment section!"

"It's different though, this is a video I put up on my own."

"All the more reason to not look. Are you having fun?"

"What?"

"Are you having fun?"

"I don't know."

"No. Listen to the words coming out of my mouth."

She brought the camera up to her face so all he could see was her eyes. "Are you enjoying working with Lindsey?"

"I guess. I mean yeah, she's cool..." and hot. He had pulled up her channel a few times since they began talking. Sure, her low cut shirts grabbed his attention, but it was more than that. Everything about her exuded confidence. She looked so comfortable in her skin—Lindsey was everything he wanted to be himself. When she looked into the camera, an electric surge shot up his spine.

"You guess? You've been talking about her nonstop since she reached out, and your voice has gone up at least an octave."

Again, with the insults. He was about to fake a bad internet connection when Genie quickly added, "It's been really nice to see. Seriously, like—even though we are trapped inside it's like you're exploring more than you ever had before. I was getting so tired of hearing the same three concerns coming out of your mouth every day. You couldn't find a job that made your grandpa happy, you were annoyed with Rufus and the club, someone brought up the video. For the first time it feels like you're actually trying to take control of your life."

"Gee, thanks."

"Don't be a dick and get defensive. I mean it. I was getting worried you were entering a point of no return before. If you're nervous now about something new it just means you're growing."

She was right. He couldn't deny that, with the exception of the most recent comments, things were starting to feel different. He hadn't drummed in over a day, and the sky hadn't fallen. Well, the world *was* coming to an end and the rapture may have only been a couple days away for all he knew, but he couldn't blame that on a lack of drumming. "You're right."

"I know I am, I always am. But it's still nice to hear."

They went on talking about their days. Genie explained that she was MIA for a while because her sister had been in the hospital after having COVID symptoms. Rick filled her in on the latest conversations with his grandpa, and as they wrapped up Genie left him with one more piece of advice. "Just because Shawn Boston's name is growing your channel, doesn't mean his brand has to overshadow you. Work with Lindsey, have fun, try something new, but if music is still what you want to do, maybe this is a blessing. I saw your other videos; all their views are up too. Just because you're working on this Shawn thing now, doesn't mean you have to give it up."

They said goodbye, and Rick pulled up the script with Lindsey's notes on it. She had changed so much without leaving any suggestions. It was clear they weren't edits so much as full on rewrites, but Rick was okay with that. He recorded the video and sent the private link to Lindsey for approval, then snuck downstairs to play. The second he sat behind his drums the rest of the world went silent. The sound of the bass put everything in perspective. Attention was coming but he was setting the terms, and with Lindsey's help he could grow. His camera steady against his textbooks, he knocked out a two hour session.

When he finished, he saw a notification from Lindsey. "No more edits!" He reread the message to be sure, and melted when he saw she sent a heart. "This is perfect! We are gonna stick it to him good." She included a selfie at a generous angle which he politely saved on his phone—the way a gentleman does.

The next two days were quiet. He was still smiling at his latest video call with Lindsey. She was incredible. The way she watched him, and complimented him. The way she wanted to see him. He had been ready to go through his entire life as a shadow because he forgot how wonderful it was to want to be seen this way. His grandpa left the apartment, and Rick still had no idea where he was going but it gave him the perfect opportunity to siphon some of his vodka. "To Shawn Boston's shittiness," Genie toasted over their video call.

"Hear, hear!" he clinked his glass against the camera, careful not to crack it. He couldn't remember the last time everything in his life felt so steady, and it only took the end of the world to get there.

His call with Genie was interrupted by an incoming message from Lindsey. Feeling more than a little tipsy from his second helping of vodka, he answered with a goofy grin on his face and attempted his most seductive "Hello there," which Lindsey responded to with three sobering words:

New Shawn Video.

Chapter 13

"I told you something like this would happen!"

Lindsey sat in her apartment, on her couch, covered in a giant blanket. She tried to imagine she was in a comfy blanket fort, but it was hard when Athena was across from her, pacing back and forth and yelling. "No, you didn't," came Lindsey's somewhat muffled reply.

"Yes, I did! Don't you remember all the warnings I gave you before you posted that goddamn video? And then the fight we had in the lobby?"

Lindsey curled up deeper in her makeshift blanket fort. "I remember being mad. But you had no way to know this would happen."

"And then on top of everything, even after all of that, you went and made *another* video with that Rick dude!"

"Rick's cute, though," Lindsey said.

Lindsey had been talking with Rick more and more since they decided to do the collab video on Shawn. After they'd filmed their pieces, they got on a Zoom call to talk about it.

The talking had quickly turned to drinking together, which quickly turned to ranting to each other about the pandemic and how much it had ruined both of their careers. For Rick the job pool dried up and for Lindsey the lack of conventions drained her savings. From there, they started getting into serious stuff.

Lindsey told Rick about her family, and how she never felt like she belonged. She told him about her brother, Tony, and how her parents liked him better because he was a consultant and made more money. She told him about her cheating ex, Chad, and how Tony had taken his side during the breakup, forcing her to move to a shitty apartment.

Rick told Lindsey about his grandpa. He poured his heart out, telling her everything, and Lindsey was more than eager to listen. While Lindsey sipped cheap white wine from a giant bottle, Rick drank from a glass of bourbon, and pretty soon they were both drunk.

Lindsey had watched through the computer monitor as Rick, slurring his words just a little, opened up about his grandparents. About how his parents hadn't been in the picture for most of his life, and how he lived through his grandparents' divorce.

He told Lindsey about his grandma leaving his grandpa for a motorcycle lesbian, and how his grandpa still got upset if anyone ever brought it up.

Then, there was a moment when a bit of drunken magic happened. Rick looked at Lindsey, and she remembered thinking how cute he was, wishing she could lean in and kiss him, and that she couldn't because they were on Zoom, and this was a pandemic. His wide eyes looked sincere. He smiled a little and said, "I just met you, but I feel like I can trust you."

Holy shit that's a lot of responsibility, Lindsey thought. But the truth was, she felt the same. So, she said, "You're one of the most genuine people I've ever met. Especially on the internet, of all places."

He replied, "I'm drunk as shit, but I feel like I trust you. Can I tell you a big secret?"

Lindsey's heart had fluttered a little when she heard that. She felt the corners of her mouth beginning to smile involuntarily. "Of course."

Rick had laughed in response. "I was... kind of a meme a few years ago."

Then, he shared his screen to show Lindsey the video of his grandpa kicking his ass.

Lindsey laughed, saying, "Oh my God, that was you? I remember this video from way back in the day!"

Rick looked a little sad when he replied, "Oh no. I was hoping you were one of the few people in the world who hadn't seen it."

Lindsey's smile fell. "Oh, I'm sorry. I didn't mean to laugh at you."

"No, it's okay," Rick smiled again. "As long as you don't judge me for it."

Lindsey shrugged and took another gulp of wine. "Hardly the weirdest thing out there on the internet, right? Plus, I didn't really get a good look at your face when I saw that video. It was so long ago and I just kind of saw it in passing. I didn't expect you to be so... adorable, I guess?"

Lindsey couldn't tell if she saw him blush or if that was just the shitty lighting on Zoom.

"Aw, thanks," he said, a little quietly. "You're, uh, pretty adorable, too."

"Thanks!" Lindsey said. "You mean like, actually adorable? Not like, show me your giant tits and I promise to buy 50 enamel pins?"

Rick took another swig of bourbon from his glass. "I didn't know that offer was on the table," he chuckled.

"You're way smoother when you're drunk on Zoom than when you're talking to me in the YouTube comment section."

"It's all the alcohol. I can already guarantee I'm going to be ridiculously embarrassed in the morning."

"Well, I guess that's a sunk cost then. Might as well enjoy the situation you've got."

From there, things got steamy.

Well, as steamy as they could over a video chat, anyway. A few times, Lindsey thought the moment was right to lean in and kiss him, causing her to feel almost a magnetic pull forward; then she'd remember that a computer screen was in front of her, not Rick's cute face.

The call quickly devolved into drunken debauchery, which included both of them removing a couple articles of clothing and talking about what they wished they could do to one another... if there wasn't a pandemic going on, of course.

"No, Rick is not cute!" Athena protested. "He's a big weenie!"

"He does have a big weenie. I saw it on Zoom."

Athena made a gagging noise in the back of her throat.

"I wish we could've done that, but there's a pandemic going on right now."

Athena grabbed a pillow off of Lindsey's bed and threw it at her. When the pillow hit her face with a *wumph* noise, she finally pulled the blanket back from her head, revealing messy, dark brown hair with pink highlights that had nearly faded back to blond. She pulled her knees up to her chest. "Seriously, Athena. I didn't think—"

"That's exactly the problem, you *didn't* think!"

Lindsey rolled her eyes. "Okay, don't cut me off with lame-ass movie cliche lines like that. What I meant was, I didn't think Shawn would ever see the video. Mine or Rick's. Or the one we made together. And if he did, I just thought maybe he'd get you some royalties or something for the art. I didn't think he'd do this."

"You didn't think he'd defend himself?"

Lindsey paused for a moment. The truth was, she just hadn't thought that far ahead at all. Everything had felt so fast-paced and unpredictable since she joined the internet influencer world.

"Well," Athena sighed, "I guess we'll just have to see what happens in the video when it releases tonight."

"Stay for a watch party, please," Lindsey begged. "Rick and his friend Genie are hopping on Zoom for a group call. All four of us can watch together."

"I don't know if I want to watch Shawn defending his own theft of *my* art," said Athena.

"But you've gotta meet Rick!"

"Are you two even dating yet? Or did you just get naked on Zoom together?"

Lindsey shrugged. "It's a pandemic. What is dating but getting naked on Zoom?"

Athena rolled her eyes again. "I just never wanted to be involved in this, that's all."

"I hate to break this to you," Lindsey said, "but you've always been involved. From long before I exposed Shawn. It was *your art* that he stole."

Athena sighed. "Okay. I'll order us some takeout and we'll make it a real watch party. How much wine do you have?"

"I've got like 15 of those $2 bottles from Trader Joe's."

"Great. Do you want pad thai?"

"Unlike you, I do not eat pad thai for every single meal. Can't we get like five pizzas?"

"We don't need five pizzas. There are only two of us."

"Yeah, but then we can have leftovers. Minimize number of deliveries. It's a pandemic, after all."

Athena rolled her eyes again, but this time with a little smile. Then she pulled out her cell phone and ordered five pizzas.

Shawn Boston's new video, titled "I Am Not an Art Thief!", was scheduled to release at seven o'clock that night. Lindsey set her laptop on the coffee table, where she and Athena sat next to each other with several open pizza boxes across the floor. They each held a slice of pizza in their hands, no plate, and watched the release timer count down on Shawn's video.

In another window, Lindsey had started the Zoom call and was waiting for Rick and his friend Genie to join.

"Hey, Lindsey!"

She clicked over to the Zoom window when she heard that familiar voice. The voice that had been saying all kinds of dirty shit to her the other night. She smiled. "Hey, Rick. Is Genie here?"

"Yes, I'm here!" came a soft female voice. No face accompanied it, though. Next to Rick's video was a square with a small, illustrated avatar: a silhouette of a woman rising out of the steam in a coffee cup. "I never turn my camera on," said Genie.

"This is Athena," Lindsey said.

"Oh, the artist? The creator of the great *Grape Nipples?*" Rick asked.

"Oh God. I never wanted anyone to know who I was!"

Athena whined, burying her face in Lindsey's throw blanket.

Then, a beeping noise emerged from Lindsey's laptop. She clicked back over to the YouTube page, where Shawn's video thumbnail now showed a countdown. The video would begin in 5... 4... 3... 2... 1...

Shawn appeared suddenly as he took a deep breath. "Hello to all my lovely friends and fans!" his voice boomed. Shawn wasn't showing off his mansion or his fancy recording studio like he often did in his vlogs. Instead, today, he was just sitting on a regular armchair in front of a plain white wall. He wasn't dressed in one of his cool hipster outfits, either. He was just wearing a plain white T-shirt and jeans, and his hair wasn't styled in a fun swoop or a pompadour like usual; today, his hair was kind of flat, slicked back just a little. He took a second deep breath. "Shawn Boston here, and I'm ready to address all the criticism I've gotten lately, to take accountability for my actions, and also to put an end to some nasty rumors that have surfaced."

"So far this seems okay," Lindsey said. "He's acting pretty normal right now. And he said he's going to take some accountability, so... maybe we're in the clear?"

Lindsey still wasn't sure what those "nasty rumors" were, though. She imagined that line might refer to some of the speculation in her comment section. She remembered that, shortly after she'd posted her first video, a lot of people had started calling Shawn a "creep" and making claims without anything to back them up. Maybe that's what he meant? Maybe his title was just clickbait after all?

"I wouldn't be so sure," Rick replied. "The internet has made me a cynical man. Let's wait and see what he says."

Shawn continued talking, his basic-ass medium-brown

hair popping against the eggshell-toned wall behind him. "First of all, as many of you know, I recently released my new album called 'Fruits of My Labor.' The reason I chose that name is because this album truly is the fruit of my labor."

"No shit," Rick said.

"I have worked harder on this album than on anything else in my entire life. I put my heart and soul into every single song. I talked about difficult things in my life, like my parents' divorce, and my struggle with leaving my hometown in Indiana, and how sometimes I still feel like that small, little country boy trying to make it in the big, mean, cutthroat city of Los Angeles."

Through her computer speakers, Lindsey heard Rick scoff a little. "He's really trying to win the audience's favor, isn't he?"

Lindsey shrugged. "I don't know. Maybe he means it?"

"Oh, come on. Don't fall for this crap."

"Yeah, you're right," Lindsey agreed.

"First and foremost, I'd like to take accountability for something," Shawn continued.

"Here it is," Athena said. "He's finally going to admit to stealing my art. I'm not sure I'm ready for—"

"I want to apologize to my fans. I know you guys were all expecting to celebrate an album, but instead all you got was drama and exposé videos. You guys know that my channel is a drama-free zone. Here on the Shawn Boston channel, we try to keep it about the music. So, I'm truly sorry if any of you had your experience tainted."

Lindsey stared at the computer screen wide-eyed. Was Shawn for real right now?

"I want to address the rumors about me stealing art. First, to all my fans, I want to assure you that I, Shawn Boston, am no art thief. A few videos have gone around claiming that I stole the work of another artist, that my album cover rips off someone else's work. That is just not true. But I want to make something else clear: I never claimed that I designed the art myself. In fact, I want to state outright that it's not my art on the cover. I do not possess those amazing painting skills to create something that beautiful. So, the channels who quote-unquote 'exposed' me, PunkKittyByLindseyDrake and BigRickEnergy, were not wrong in that aspect. What they said was true: I didn't design that art myself. However, I never stole the art either."

"That was never my criticism of him, though!" Lindsey yelled at the computer screen. "I never accused Shawn of 'not making the art himself.' No one ever thought he painted his own album covers! He's completely—"

"Strawmanning? Avoiding the actual argument to make himself sound like the good guy?" Rick interjected. "Yeah, that sounds like a classic manipulator."

Lindsey gripped her hair and flopped her head backwards on the couch in despair.

Meanwhile, Shawn continued his monologue. "My production team at BigD Studios designed that art for me. They took me through the entire process from the idea's conception to the completed product. Actually, the painting itself was done by my good friend Elise Shiloh."

Lindsey felt a slight shift on the couch next to her. She lifted her head up from the back of the couch and looked at Athena, who was now sitting frozen in her seat, her face in her hands. Her eyes were wide, but she was silent.

"But I am not mad at these two other creators, Rick and Lindsey," Shawn continued. "The truth is, I'm grateful for people like them. In today's cutthroat world, it's important that we have people who still care about standing up for their friends, about standing up for art and for music. I think that deep down, Rick, and Lindsey are good people. They just missed the mark on this one. In fact, I believe that maybe this girl, Lindsey's friend, actually did create art that looked a lot like my album cover. And I know how important it is to support smaller creators. I wish I could link that artist in my description below, because I'd love to help her gain some followers. If her art really does look similar to my album cover, I'll bet her work is beautiful. Unfortunately, I've watched Lindsey's video in full, and I've learned that this artist doesn't really have an online presence, so I'm not able to promote her. But, Lindsey…"

Shawn stared directly at his camera as he addressed Lindsey. Lindsey watched Shawn's eyes staring right at her. She felt her fingers go numb as he addressed her directly.

"Lindsey, if your friend ever does create a store online, please know that my offer still stands. I will support her. Because we're all artists in this world. Right now, especially in the midst of a pandemic that's threatening all of our jobs and lives, we need to be supporting one another, not making exposé videos to tear each other down. That's about all I have to say on this matter. I love you all so much."

Then the video ended.

"Well," Rick sighed, "that was the most manipulative thing I've ever seen."

Lindsey took a deep breath and relaxed her tensed shoulders. "Yeah," she agreed, nodding a little. "Yeah, honestly, that whole video was bullshit."

"He tried so hard to make himself look like the good guy. And what sucks is that people are going to fall for it," Rick said.

"Who is *he* to go on about the pandemic threatening our jobs and lives? You know who *actually* lost jobs in the pandemic?"

"I did," said Rick.

"Shawn sure didn't," Lindsey continued.

"He 1,000% used that as a way to deflect criticism."

"And here's the thing. We *know* Elise didn't design it. Athena did. We know Athena sent it to Elise. We have proof!"

"You have proof? Like... receipts?" Rick asked.

Lindsey nodded. Athena shifted on the couch next to her, looking uneasy.

"I saw Athena email a digital print of that painting to Elise back in February. Elise was holding a contest to feature some new artists during her big presentation at ArtCon. But maybe her whole contest was really a front to siphon some art to plagiarize for Shawn's album."

"Lindsey, if you have proof, we need to go public with it! Shawn's a lying asshole and the world needs to know."

"We can't!" Athena interjected.

Lindsey turned away from Rick's face on her laptop screen and looked at Athena. "Athena, I know that you don't want your name out there publicly. But we might need to—"

"No, we don't need to! I didn't want to be involved in this!"

Lindsey flopped back on the couch.

"Hey, uh, guys?" Genie's voice came from the laptop, her avatar picture lighting up.

"What's up, Genie?" Rick asked.

"Rick, Lindsey, have either of you checked your YouTube channels since Shawn's new video went up?"

"What do you mean 'since his video went up'?" Rick asked. "His video went up, like, five minutes ago!"

"Five minutes is fast on the internet," said Genie.

Lindsey pulled her phone out of her back pocket and

opened the YouTube app. A nervous wave of heat washing over her, she checked her notifications.

500 new comments, just in the past five minutes.

And her subscriber count was rapidly dropping.

"So, it turns out you lied about the whole thing?" the first comment read.

"You were just bullying Shawn all along because you don't like him!"

"You were just another one of Shawn's haters the whole time!"

These comments made no sense to Lindsey; until she knew Shawn had plagiarized Athena's art, she'd actually been a big fan. And she hadn't lied about anything; she just hadn't shown full proof without Athena's permission. Plus, she was confused about the whole "another one of Shawn's haters" thing; until Lindsey and Rick had put out their first exposé videos a couple weeks ago, Shawn didn't seem to have *any* haters, at least on a large public scale. In fact, most of Lindsey's comments on that first video had been thanking her for being the first one to speak out about Shawn's true nature.

She groaned. This sucked, but she couldn't help herself; she kept reading.

"I hope you enjoyed your massive channel growth for lying about Shawn. It'll all be gone soon."

"I can't believe I not only subscribed to your channel, but bought your art too. I was such a big fan of you, Punk-Kitty. And now it turns out you were just bullying Shawn for attention!"

"Never trust a YouTube channel with their own links in the description. PunkKitty was clearly just trying to capitalize on a hot topic like Shawn to get more traffic to her own online store."

"PunkKitty is a DrawmaLlamas wannabe. You just

wanted a piece of their popularity, so you lied about Shawn!!!"

"You got so mad about Shawn supposedly 'stealing' your 'friend's' art, yet all you do is copy the type of videos the DrawmaLlamas make!"

"Who wants to bet PunkKitty's friend doesn't even exist?"

Lindsey sighed loudly and threw her phone on the coffee table. "I can't read any more of these!"

Athena shrugged a little. "I kind of like the comment that says it doesn't think I exist."

"Your comments are that bad too, huh?" Rick said.

"I had to stop reading Rick's comment section after the first few," Genie added.

"How are we going to fix this?" Lindsey groaned.

"You don't have to fix it," Athena said. "It's just the internet. You're able to log off like everyone else. Just delete your YouTube channel and stick to other methods of learning online marketing for the meantime. I found this new course online about how to sell when socially distanced, you could—"

"Oh my God, Athena, you're not still buying business courses, are you? After Elise blatantly stole your art and gave it to Shawn Boston? You still trust these sleazy business coaches?"

"Well, yesterday I learned from a new course all about how to set up a PayPal account," Athena bragged.

"Everyone already has a PayPal account. You don't need a course for that."

"Yeah, but with a PayPal account, I can have people transfer me money for my art, and then I can mail it to them. I'm having my grandma mail out flyers to people, and then they can call me on the phone to place an order."

"Oh my God, Athena, just use the internet already!" Lindsey yelled.

"It's my choice not to."

"Guys, stop fighting! We can fix this!" Rick shouted.

"What do you mean?" Lindsey asked.

"Well, Shawn's new video is full of lies about everything that happened, right? We have the proof that Athena sent this art to Elise in the first place, but Athena doesn't want to show it and that's okay. That's her right. But we don't even need to show the receipts. Shawn dug his own grave in his video without even realizing it!"

Lindsey scooted forward on the couch, leaning her head in closer to her laptop, closer to Rick's adorable face. "Tell me more!"

"While you guys were arguing about PayPal and placing orders on the phone—by the way, Athena, Lindsey's right about that, it's not 1990, okay? Anyway, while you were arguing, I watched Shawn's video a second time. In it, he made a crucial mistake; he said that his *production team* created the art. Sure, he falsely claimed that Elise painted it herself, which we can't prove without Athena's help, but even if we can't prove *that*, we can call out his *production team*."

Lindsey nodded. "I think I'm starting to get it. Shawn's never mentioned a production team in any of his videos before—"

"—because he's built his entire image on being super indie and super dedicated to the music—"

"—and his journey from a small town boy from buttfuck nowhere Indiana to a music star all on his own—"

"—but he just revealed that he has a whole team behind him at BigD Studios, which is a huge corporation—"

"—so, we can expose that he's still a liar!"

Athena arched an eyebrow. "Wow, you two are really on the same wavelength. Hearing you finish each other's sentences is making me want to vomit."

"We're cute together, aren't we?" Lindsey smiled.

"Aw, thanks," Rick said shyly through the computer.

"And for our next date, let's expose Shawn Boston together!"

Chapter 14

"I can't believe he did this. Call me back, please." Rick left Genie a voicemail, his mind still reeling from the previous evening's events.

"Don't read the comments, don't read the comments," he repeated to himself, but those words were as useful as a strainer on a sinking ship. Of course, his eyes darted from link to link and read the replies laughing at him.

"This is the guy calling out Shawn?"

"What a loser!"

"Shoulda smacked him harder and taught him some manners."

"WEAK TRIGGERED WEAK."

Things weren't moving fast enough. Lindsey seemed to have a plan, or at least wore the confidence of a person who had one, but Rick wanted to see results now. He wanted to release something that could turn all of those comments into crying emojis. How could they love an artist who stole from another? It was so much more than a product, as Elise Shiloh loved to put it. When someone created something that hadn't previously existed in the world it was a part of them. Rick didn't believe in a god or anything, but music felt like a part of his soul. The way the drums vibrated off the walls like a heart brought him life, and Shawn wanted to steal that experience from someone for a profit—for money he didn't even need and a reputation that couldn't be destroyed.

Rick joined the Zoom call, and from the jump he kept glancing down at Lindsey's low cut shirt. Every two words he froze to get another glimpse. He knew it was pathetic, but he couldn't help himself. Either way she didn't seem to mind. She had written most of the script while he drooled like a fool. He felt like part of a team when they talked without video. Then he could at least make it a whole sentence without losing his train of thought.

"You think you can finish your half this afternoon?" she asked.

"My half?" he didn't know what she meant by that. He could have the whole thing done in under an hour with the way he usually edited. Lindsey's videos would take him a degree and a half to understand. He was excited when he learned the picture-in-picture function. She had sound effects, popping animations, zoom ins, pans, and other transitions he couldn't find in his laptop's video editor program.

"Just send me what you can, and I'll finish the rest." She hung up before he could say another word. Rick rested his hands on his stomach—the situation had gotten serious, and his entire being had never felt heavier. Lindsey was carrying them, and the fact he was so useless he couldn't even help if he tried made him feel weak. He couldn't make out the words on the script and kept restarting his intro because he would lose his place halfway through.

"Damnit!" he clapped his hands and prepared for take number 12. She didn't need him to do much, but he struggled to even do that. "Come on," he tried to psyche himself up. This time he made it halfway through the script before sneezing. His eyes watered and he couldn't make out anything else, finally pausing the take and dropping to the floor. He rested his face in his hands and tried to calm himself. It was all going to be okay. He knew he shouldn't have taken it so hard, but he kept falling back on Shawn's video. How could someone so fake be so loved? What drew people to him? Were we inclined to always gravitate towards fiction because we hoped one day our lives would be consumed by it? Watch enough tv and you can step through the screen, read enough books and the covers will snap around you, listen to enough music and you'll fly away on the melody.

Maybe that was the problem with his life. He was too real. Most of the time when someone took the microphone, they got stage fright. Or when they wore the gloves, they got knocked out. Most "first times" end with an early climax and at least 50% of the audience unsatisfied. He was trapped in a looping Boomerang of reality on everyone else's Instagram feed as a reminder of what trying to jump into fiction could do to a person, whereas Shawn gave them the chance to experience it without the risk.

He sat back up and waited for his eyes to adjust, letting the anger stew. Since Lindsey entered his life, he saw a path out of his tunnel. He no longer had to hide in the shadows produced by the spotlight, but could follow it back into the audience— or maybe to another stage altogether. All he had to do was take her lead.

He let the words flow from his mouth the way Lindsey would have spoken them. He paused to collect his thoughts instead of stuttering over his "ums," and he even looked at the camera, locking eyes with the audience.

He cut it down as best he could on his phone and sent it off to Lindsey. He hadn't realized how much ad money he was piling up. He still hadn't received a payment from YouTube, so he never bothered to check, but Lindsey's excitement over Shawn's negative attention started to make more sense. Even the dislikes on his videos from Shawn fans were driving traffic up, and traffic was all that mattered to the company paying him.

Chapter 15

Lindsey couldn't cool off after Zoom sex. She sat there naked in her desk chair, staring at Rick through the video chat call, still panting and sweaty. Maybe it was too soon to make the call—and maybe her brain was still too flooded with endorphins to think clearly—but that *might have been* the best sex she'd ever had; and they didn't even physically touch.

It was definitely better than all the sex she'd had with dumb-fuck Chad. When Lindsey had first learned Chad was cheating on her with all those women at the coffee shop, she remembered feeling surprised; not because Chad was cheating (part of her had always known he was an asshole), but because he was able to snag that much pussy in the first place. Chad was terrible at sex. He liked to fall asleep right after she finished sucking his dick. And damn, he was so bad at eating pussy it was laughable. Rick making stupid cunnilingus faces at the webcam did more for Lindsey than Chad haphazardly bopping his tongue in her vagina's general direction.

"Is this us now?" Lindsey asked Rick with a laugh,

staring at the computer. "Is canceling Shawn Boston our foreplay?"

Rick laughed. "I guess so. And somehow, it's not even the weirdest thing that's happened in 2020."

"Not by far."

They both laughed a little.

Lindsey's phone buzzed on her desk.

"If we want to get really kinky with it," Rick said, "we could make a million exposé videos, and then you can just hold your phone against your vagina while it vibrates nonstop with notifications."

"That is so brilliant it hurts," Lindsey said, picking up her phone and checking the new notifications. "I think you're onto something, Rick," she continued, scrolling through the comment section of their new YouTube video about Shawn. "At least some people are back on our side again."

"Nice," said Rick.

"God, I'm still so horny," she continued.

"Was it not enough?" Rick asked, suddenly sounding worried.

"Oh, no, everything we did was great! But, uh," she swallowed, "I know this sounds weird, but... I think I get aroused by attention."

"Attention?"

"Yeah. So, like... seeing people loving our video, seeing all the comments roll in... it's turning me on again." She gave a slight, mischievous smile.

Rick laughed. "I can't say I understand how that feels at all, but I could get into it if you're saying you want a round two."

"I might be down for a round two if you are."

On the computer screen, Lindsey watched Rick grab his massive dick once again. But before they could begin, her phone buzzed loudly... and continuously this time. A phone call. "Athena's calling me," she said. "That's weird. She lives upstairs. She usually just comes down to the apartment."

"Well, it's probably better that she doesn't right now, since, you know, you're naked."

Lindsey shrugged. "I'm naked most of the time." She swiped her finger across the screen to answer. "Hey, what's up?"

"I tried logging onto YouTube for just a minute," Athena said.

"Oh, so you *do* know how to use the internet, little miss tsundere," Lindsey teased.

"Um, you might want to stop banging Rick or jerking off to yourself or whatever you're doing right now for just a second. Shawn released a surprise new single. Thought you might want to read the comments."

Lindsey dropped her phone on the desk. "Thanks, Athena," she sighed, and ended the call.

"What was that about?" Rick asked.

"While we were having socially distanced sex, Shawn apparently dropped a new song. Out of nowhere."

"What?" said Rick. "How did he do that so fast? Unless, like we said, he has a whole production team behind him."

Lindsey pulled up her YouTube page alongside the Zoom call and shared her screen with Rick. She typed "Shawn Boston" in the search bar, then arrived on his channel, where he had a new video posted just 20 minutes ago. "Surprise new single: Indie in Indiana."

"Oh, he's fucking with us now," Lindsey said. "What else could he possibly be doing?"

"If nothing else, 'Indie in Indiana' is one of the shittiest song titles I've ever heard."

Lindsey clicked on the video, and the two of them listened together.

"Hello, lovely friends and fans! Shawn Boston here with a surprise song! I decided to go back to my roots for this one. As many of you know, I may look like a big music star from the outside, but deep down, I always feel like I'm still that little boy from rural Indiana, just having big dreams. And that's why I'm proud to be an indie musician who does everything myself. Here's my new song, with just me and my acoustic guitar, 'Indie in Indiana.'"

Then, Shawn launched into his mediocre song, which had lyrics about his humble upbringing and multiple chord progressions that were obvious rip-offs of "Wonderwall."

"This song *sucks*," Rick complained. "Everything in it sounds like a bad cover of one of those whiny early 2000s boy bands."

"The comment section seems to love it, though," Lindsey said, scrolling down through his comments.

Lots of Shawn's fans replied with things like:

"I'm so glad you didn't listen to those stupid haters. BigRick and PunkKitty have no idea what they're talking about. You're an inspiration, Shawn!"

"I live in Indiana too! You make me feel like I can truly follow my dreams! Thank you, Shawn!"

"I love how this video is so classy yet still STICKS IT to those stupid haters, Rick and Lindsey!! You didn't even have to call them out, you just SHOWED them that you're truly indie with the POWER OF MUSIC."

Lindsey soaked up the negative attention. "All right," she said. "So, we can plan our next clap back. But first, let's do round two."

"You still want to have sex again?" Rick asked. "While we're publicly being insulted by thousands of people?"

"Yeah. I'm actually even hornier than before," she said.

"I'm getting so wet I'm actually worried I might damage this desk chair."

Rick stared at her, a little confused. "But I thought you got turned on by all the praise from the comment section. And from seeing your sub counts rise and all that."

Lindsey shrugged. "Dude, go into Shawn's comment section and hit 'control-F' and search our names. We're each mentioned like, hundreds of times!" Her breath came out heavy at the end of that sentence.

"Wait, the *negative* comments turn you on, too?!" Rick's eyes grew wide.

"Well, yeah, why wouldn't they?"

"I don't know," said Rick. "They seem kind of hurtful."

"It's all attention either way," said Lindsey. And for the purposes of sex, attention is what gets me going. That and your monster cock."

Rick blushed a little. "Oh, uh, thanks."

"That's cute," Lindsey giggled. "How you can stay flustered like that even after I've literally seen your dick on a Zoom call. You're adorable, Rick."

He laughed nervously. "Thanks. You too. I mean, you're super hot. But also, like... Right now, I'm feeling kind of..."

"Horny?"

"No. I mean, don't get me wrong, that was super hot what you did earlier, when you made me cum on the webcam."

"Watching you clean it off was the cherry on top," Lindsey said with a smile.

"It was hot as hell, actually. This is the best sexual experience I've had since college. But right now, I don't know. I'm just feeling kind of sad I guess."

"Why?"

"What do you mean *why*? Maybe because hundreds of

people are shit-talking us on one of the internet's most popular YouTube channels?"

Lindsey nodded.

"Sorry, I'm just... having trouble getting hard when all I can think of is Shawn Boston's smug-ass stupid face."

"I mean, Shawn Boston's pretty hot, too. Even if he's an asshole," said Lindsey.

"Okay, and with that, I am leaving this call," said Rick.

"Wait, I didn't mean it like—"

But it was too late. Rick had signed off, leaving Lindsey alone, staring at her own naked body on her computer screen.

And for the first time in a long time, maybe her whole life, Lindsey wondered if she'd gone too far.

Chapter 16

Lindsey wasn't wrong, attention paid well. Maybe Grandpa wouldn't have to suck dick for roof. At this rate, he could even save up for a new computer, and it didn't matter that none of his job searches yielded interviews. His phone buzzed in his pocket, and he silenced it.

The more negative attention he got, the less it fazed him, but she constantly spoke over him, and actively sought the anger. It was one thing to not be afraid of a mugging, and another to dare someone with a gun to do it.

Again, his phone buzzed and again he silenced it. While he wasn't hiding in a ball each time, he saw a comment bringing up his infamous viral video, he could never bring himself to reply. It was the main point they all brought up against him, and the only solace he found was that the first ad payment looked like it would be more than he made in three months at Low Octave. But what good was more money if everyone would just recognize him as the loser again? It felt like COVID was the only thing stopping him from being laughed at.

"And are we going to forget who this clown going after

Shawn is?" The speaker, who went by iLuvShawn69 on YouTube, cut to a clip of Rick's infamous viral video. When he watched himself hit the ground he still winced, and it didn't help that all the videos attacking him added sound effects with each strike. Lindsey insisted it was great for their growth—the more people hate-watched, the more money they made. It was simple math and he hated it.

For a third time his phone vibrated against his leg, he pulled it out to see Genie had been calling him, but he didn't have time, so he flipped his phone over and ignored her once more.

"They're funding the anti-Shawn Boston movement," she chuckled. He saw her point, but it wasn't the easiest pill to swallow. Yes, the more attention they got the more money it reeled in, but the videos were more than words to Rick. It was five years he could never get back, and the more they made the smaller his world felt.

iLuvShawn69 jabbed his finger against his desk with each point he made about Rick and Lindsey, which was a reaction Rick had never gotten before. They saw him as a threat. Before this internet drama, the reactions he elicited were laughter and selfies. Conversations were had in his presence without a single word spoken. But now they were sending waves of dislikes to his channel—and new subscribers. The likes and positive comments were going up, too.

"You're right man!"

"Dead on the money!"

"Been saying he's a phony for years!"

He had never experienced that before. Being a meme meant nothing but laughter. Being a target of anger elicited support.

His phone buzzed, and he saw Lindsey's name, so he flipped it over. She only cared about him for his dick or the money. Still, a hollow feeling grew in his stomach. No one ever made him feel as special as she had, and he didn't want to cut her off entirely, but how could he tell if she wanted him, or just wanted attention.

Flipping the phone back over, he saw Lindsey had sent a text. "Collab soon?"

That was it, another collaboration? Was that all they were going to do now? He had said all he needed to about Shawn with the last video—what more was there to say? They called him out for being a fake, and stealing cover art. He didn't need to research his entire background or team. He was ready to move on to the next thing with his channel.

Rick took a deep breath and deleted his one word response. It all went back to Shawn. He wasn't a star for his shine. Everyone orbited around him: fans, haters, people asking "who the fuck is Shawn Boston?" Life swirled around him until all other life was unsustainable, and continuing down this road with Lindsey guaranteed that if he ever did break away, his existence would be dark, cold, and starved of all resources. Did she actually like him, or did she just want to collaborate with him? Maybe she didn't see him as anything more than an asset—a means to views. It was how she saw Shawn.

And if she only saw him as a person to collaborate with, then what did that mean for their relationship? Maybe to her their talks meant nothing, but he had never had a girl want him the way she said she did. Was that fake, too? Was she like his grandpa, trading sex for favors? And did that make him more pathetic than Sven for accepting?

He remembered the experience as vividly as the fight itself. Rick wore his grandpa's blazer and tie and arrived thirty minutes early, and the M&T branch manager invited him back into his office. Rather than asking Rick to take a seat, he asked him to look at something and waved Rick to his seat behind the desk. It felt like the guy was about to flash him, but this was worse. The video with his grandpa was full screen on his monitor.

"An intern recognized you the moment you came in. What happened here?" he asked. Rick tried to chuckle, but his voice abandoned him. He felt dizzy and leaned on the desk trying to keep his balance. More questions followed but he didn't hear anything except "are you okay?"

He said he just needed some air, but he went out to his car and sat in the driver seat for twenty minutes, trembling. Unable to bring himself back inside, he drove home; when his grandpa asked what happened, he couldn't tell him the truth. It was one of the first interviews he got after graduating. His grandpa was so sure a business degree would set him up for life, but so far, the closest he got to getting a job was being asked about the viral video. He couldn't bring that up to his grandpa. What would he know about being a laughingstock? He would just tell Rick to toughen up and stop blaming his problems on everyone else. But Rick wasn't blaming his problems on everyone else—just on grandpa.

He woke up to a dozen messages from Lindsey and a matching amount of calls, but he had said all he needed to. She wanted him to be a human shield. To take all the hate and video reactions so his fans were too tired or distracted to deal with her. He was an easier target, and he was done eating bullets for that psycho slut.

It needed to end, and the only way he could think of accomplishing that was pulling the plug on his channel. It would take some time for things to get back to the way they were before he ever met Lindsey, but if he kept his head down long enough, he felt like he could get there.

His phone was about to die so he pulled up his computer. Just trying to go to the website was enough to trigger a spinning wheel of death. His phone went black, and his computer froze. Plugging it in to charge, he left his room and entered the empty apartment. He wasn't surprised his grandpa was gone, most likely working for rent without even leaving the building.

He needed something sweet. Fuck COVID, and fuck his grandpa for not accepting any of his work money. He grabbed his wallet, mask, and keys before walking out. The door to the basement was open so he figured he couldn't go down to drum out his stress either.

The streets were empty. Could he have slept through the apocalypse? Or maybe it happened slowly while he was quarantined. He saw the daily case counts online, but numbers on a screen were different than looking out at the empty road. Even Allen Street, which was usually full of teens pretending to be 21 and fifty-year-olds pretending to be 22, had more cats than people on it. A ginger cat on a low brick wall walked beside Rick on his way to the corner store. *Did cats have WiFi, too?* he wondered.

He kept walking, not wanting to enter the same shop from before the lockdown. It would make that girl's day if he walked back in there again. Even with a mask on she would be able to point him out, so he went to Rite Aid. Only the cashier was inside, and he was too busy looking at his phone to notice someone walk in. For all Rick knew he had been there since before the lockdowns, and no one told him his shift was over.

He checked the prices of every piece of candy, measuring it beside the mental digits of his bank account in his head. He still hadn't been paid by YouTube yet and could practically hear the loose change in his account bouncing around like unpopped corn kernels, but he needed something. He grabbed a couple bucks worth of junk food, and walked up to the register. At first, the guy behind the counter started scanning his stuff without looking away from his phone.

He could be Rick's new best friend. Dave was a nice name, easy to remember. And Dave spoke the right amount. His long, unkempt beard was a sign of a real lockdown champ who embraced the comforts of isolation and was the perfect complement for his equally long, messy hair.

When he finally looked up, though, Rick noticed Dave's quick double take. "Wait a second, I recognize you." His eyes turned up in a smile and Rick backed away, his drink still in his hands. "*Fuck, not another selfie,*" he thought.

"You're the guy who called out Shawn."

"Wait, what?"

"This is you right?" he turned his phone around and held it up for Rick to see. It wasn't the viral video but his recent exposé video. "I was so pumped when I saw this, I've been obsessed with this take down. You and Punk Titty are doing the Lord's work as far as I'm concerned." He crossed his chest and pressed his palms together, looking briefly toward the heavens.

Rick didn't correct him on the name, half wishing Lindsey was there to hear it for herself.

"Yeah—yeah that's me." He was waiting for the second video to come up. One couldn't watch his exposé video without seeing a response, and in the response, there was always a clip of his grandpa flipping him.

"Shawn sounds like a total fuck boy. It's one thing to be a piece of shit, but stealing art, man? Art? I think I'd have more respect for him if it were an organ."

It felt like a bit of a jump, and as relieved as Rick was to have a fan, he wasn't sure he wanted to be friends with Dave anymore. Not unless he needed an organ transplant. "You heard the new album then?"

"Some of it, but if I wanted to torture myself, I'd sit on a grill during a tailgate," he laughed at his own joke, which Rick didn't understand but smiled at, not wanting to leave his not-friend out to dry. He reached for the candy, nervous that if he made too abrupt of a movement, he'd lose a hand. "Oh right, here," he tossed the chocolate bar. "On me." He pulled out his wallet. "Seriously, just seeing Shawn stammer on his last stream was worth it. You're making this lockdown bearable."

Not wanting to question the potential organ thief, he thanked Dave and left. When he was back out in the empty street with the company of the ginger cat, the reality of the situation sunk in. That wasn't a friend in there, it was a fan. He had a fan. Not someone who wanted his picture for some wall of shame or a freshman who just failed an exam and needed a reminder that their life could be worse. A real fan who valued the work he chose to put out there.

As Rick made his way toward his apartment, he noticed Sven's office door was slightly open. He walked through his front door and looked around—the apartment was still empty. He sat at his computer, finishing the last few bites of his snack. The spinning wheel was still in the center of the screen, but at least his phone was on now. As he pulled up his account, he realized he'd lost the energy to delete the videos. Dave said he made his lockdown bearable. He was laughing at Shawn. There were actually people out there who saw Rick and Shawn at the same time and sided with the chubby, unemployed drummer.

Even the individual videos now seemed to pop off the screen in a new light. How long had the likes outweighed the dislikes? And the number of supportive comments continued to grow. Each one represented another Dave, stuck at home, finally seeing Shawn get called out for the crap he tries to pull.

He pulled up his email app to clear out some of the notification emails, but as soon as he opened it the words "Monthly Transfer" stared him dead in the eyes. *This can't be real.* His first YouTube check had arrived. Those kernels echoing in his empty bank account weren't just rattling around in there anymore. They were *popping*; his wallet was quickly filling up with movie theater butter.

$1,650? It was even more than he expected. Where was the money coming from? He looked at the breakdown. While the bulk was from his Shawn videos, he completely forgot that his music videos were monetized too. Lindsey may have been right. It wasn't his entire life, but it was the means to make a life for himself.

"Grandpa!" he shouted, though he knew his apartment was empty. He ran downstairs, knowing exactly where Sven was. He could pay him directly and ask where his grandpa was. He wanted to share the news.

When he barged into Sven's office, his grandpa jumped to his feet and his equally old landlord rushed to pull up his pants.

"What the hell are you doing?" his grandpa asked abruptly.

Sven laughed and patted Phil on the shoulder, but he shrugged the landlord off and stomped towards Rick, who held his phone up. "I came to talk to Sven I swear."

"Always happy to talk to ya sport," he opened his arms wide, but the last thing Rick wanted to do was walk into an embrace with someone who'd been... enjoying life the way he was moments earlier.

"It's about rent."

"I thought I told you to stop worrying about it, I've gotten it taken care of." His grandpa gave an insistent stare.

Rick's throat tightened. He tried not to gag, but he didn't need to think about his grandpa *taking care of* rent.

"I just thought, maybe now you wouldn't have to."

Sven's smile somehow grew. "That's so sweet. Phil, you have such a lovely grandchild. I'm sure you're awfully proud."

"That's one word for it."

"But he is right, your rent is all taken care of for the next few months, no one is getting kicked out during a lockdown."

"Yes, but I just want—I mean, wait, what?"

"Jesus Christ, did you think I was doing this *for rent?*" his grandpa replied, now looking horrified.

"He was just concerned for you Phil." Sven tried to put a hand on Phil's shoulder again.

Phil shrugged it off. "What kinda person do you think I am—or him? What, do you think we lack all decency?"

"I just wanted—"

"To help, and I understand that." Sven stepped between the two and looked at the green Rick was holding out. "Impressive, where have you been working?"

"It's from, uh—it's from my videos." Rick pulled at his collar sheepishly.

"Your videos? Your talent surprises me more by the day. Still, don't worry about rent, not for now anyway. Set that money aside, save it for when you really need something, or buy something that makes this lockdown a little more bearable. We could all use a little break right now, couldn't we?" he smiled back at Phil who folded his arms and looked away.

Rick backed out of the room. "I guess I'll see ya later," he said, but his grandpa didn't reply. As he climbed the steps to the apartment, he thought about texting Lindsey. Even if she was right, her words echoing in his ears felt like thumb tacks poking at him. Besides, she probably wasn't too keen on him at the moment. It could've been worse; at least ten more offensive insults swirled in his head when he called her a psycho. Regardless, he doubted she wanted to hear from him.

He texted Genie instead.

"Can you talk?"

Chapter 17

"Hey, Lindsey. It's me. I want to talk. I hope you'll hear me out."

That was the subject line on the email Lindsey saw on her phone a week after Rick had stormed out of their Zoom sex call.

Her phone didn't say who the email was from. Just a notification saying: NEW EMAIL: "Hey, Lindsey. It's me. I want to talk. I hope you'll hear me out."

But that had to be Rick, right? Who else could it be? Who else could she have pissed off in the past few weeks without realizing it?

The subject line just popped up in Lindsey's notifications while she was sitting at her desk that Saturday morning. She meant to spend the day working on a new art design for Punk Kitty, but once again, she'd gotten distracted falling down the rabbit hole of Shawn Boston's comment sections.

She read all the comments, positive and negative. Then, she went over to Rick's newest videos to read those comments as well. Scrolling through the sea of opinionated keyboard warriors, she couldn't help herself: she held down the "control" and "F" keys, then typed her names in the search bar that popped up—both "Lindsey" and "Punk-Kitty." And, just as she suspected, there were hundreds of results.

"When are you and Lindsey gonna collab again? I love you 2 together!"

"BigRick & PunkKitty just have such strong energy!! I love their whole VIBE!"

"Name a MORE ICONIC DUO than BigRick & PunkKitty!"

"Not gonna lie. I kind of ship Rick & Lindsey. Would it be weird if I wrote a fanfiction about them?"

Of course, she also checked Rick's replies to the comments, most of which were unsurprisingly lackluster.

"When are you and Lindsey gonna collab again? I love you 2 together!" "Thanx. I'm not sure."

"BigRick & PunkKitty just have strong energy!! I love their whole VIBE!" "Cool."

"Name a MORE ICONIC DUO than BigRick & PunkKitty." "I don't know. Penn & Teller probably."

"Not gonna lie. I kind of ship Rick & Lindsey. Would it be weird if I wrote a fanfiction about them?" "Yeah, that'd be pretty weird."

Lindsey sighed. Rick hadn't answered any of her texts over the last week. A few days ago, on Wednesday evening, Lindsey and Athena had gotten takeout together in her apartment, drank wine, and talked about what happened.

"I don't get what I did wrong," Lindsey had told Athena.

"How do you not get it?" asked Athena, spreading out four sushi rolls on plastic trays across Lindsey's coffee table.

"I was just trying to go for round two."

"No, you weren't *just* anything. Dude, you told him that you get off on *negative* attention too?"

"Yeah. What's wrong with that? Don't kink-shame me."

Athena shrugged, working her chopsticks between her fingers to bring a California roll up to her mouth. "Some kinks are worth shaming."

"Don't think I forgot about that time last year when you got really drunk and told me that you stuck a sharpie in your butt."

Athena almost choked. "Dude, I told you not to bring that up!"

"Well, then don't kink shame me for getting turned on by negative YouTube comments!"

Athena swallowed her piece of sushi, washing it down with some wine straight out of the bottle. Lindsey and Athena each had their own bottle of two-dollar Trader Joe's chardonnay. There was a pandemic going on, after all; can't just go around sharing wine bottles. Safety first. "Fair enough," said Athena, taking a second swig of wine. "I won't kink shame you. But I will say, not everyone's into attention as much as you are. Have you considered that for Rick, this excessive attention, especially of the negative variety, might just be getting to him? Not everyone wants to fuck when they're sad."

Lindsey had remembered Athena *specifically* being sad when she'd stuck the sharpie in her butt last year, but decided not to bring that up.

"And then," Athena continued, gripping another piece of sushi between two chopsticks, "on top of everything else, you had to go and say you thought Shawn Boston was hot?"

"It was mostly a joke," said Lindsey. "I mean, Shawn's objectively attractive, but it's not like I even know Shawn

or would cheat on Rick with him or anything. I don't
understand where the jealousy came from."

"You are so dense," Athena said. "Shawn Boston was
the direct cause of Rick being so sad after you had sex.
And then you said he was hot? I'm shocked this isn't
making sense for you."

"I guess I hadn't thought of it that way," Lindsey said,
dunking her California roll in a plastic cup of soy sauce.

"Not everyone is as... exhibitionistic... as you are,"
said Athena.

Lindsey giggled. "Says the girl who paints nudes for a
living."

"Yeah, but they're not *my* nudes!" Athena giggled back.

Lindsey stopped laughing long enough to sigh with
exasperation. "So how can I fix this? I really like Rick. I
know you think he's kind of lame—"

"No, he's not that lame," Athena said.

"But last week—"

"Last week I hadn't really gotten to know him yet. He
does seem like a cool guy. I see why you like him."

"So how do I fix this?"

"I know this is going to be so, so hard for your extro-
verted ass," Athena said, "But honestly, I think you're
going to have to give him time."

So that's what Lindsey had spent the last few days
doing. Giving Rick space. She hadn't called or texted him.
She hadn't even responded to any of his YouTube
comments that mentioned her name, no matter how much
she wanted to jump into a conversation that was so obviously about her.

Now she was sitting at her desk on Saturday morning,
staring at a notification that very well might be from Rick:
"I want to talk. I hope you'll hear me out."

Did he want to talk about what happened last week?

What caused him to angrily leave the call? Was he going to give her a chance to apologize—or was *he* maybe even going to apologize?

Nervously, Lindsey opened up the notification to see the email.

But it wasn't from Rick.

No, this was an entirely different kind of email. Right there, in the "From" spot, sat an unmistakable name: Shawn Boston.

To: Lindsey Drake
From: Shawn Boston

Subject: Hey, Lindsey. It's me. I want to talk. I hope you'll hear me out.

Lindsey, hi. It's Shawn Boston. This might seem like a strange email to get, especially since we've never interacted one on one before. Also, I've heard that on the internet, you're not supposed to engage with your haters. But I kind of think that's bullshit, you know? Most haters are just friends you haven't made yet. Isn't that a saying somewhere? Anyway, I was hoping we could talk. I totally understand if you don't want to, but I'd like to make things right. Don't get me wrong; I didn't steal your friend's art, and I will never confess to doing something I didn't do. But contrary to what some might think, I do care about supporting artists. When I say in my videos that I started as a nobody in Butt-Fuck Indiana, well, I'm not lying. I had people supporting me and encouraging me to get me where I want to be. I know the kinds of hours you and your friends put into your art, and I don't want you to ever think I don't respect what you do. Anyway, since your videos have never given the name of the artist, you're claiming I stole from, or any link to her actual work, I decided to look up your work. Dude, PunkKitty is cute. The enamel pins are adorable, and I have so many friends who would like those. Anyway, I think you have a cute cartoony style that evokes a certain feeling. What I'm trying to say is, I'd like to commission you. Partially to bury the hatchet, but also because I just legitimately like your work. I'm working on another new album and need some cover art. The album's predicted to sell pretty well—as long as you don't cancel me again first, LOL—so I can pay really well. Reply if interested. Thanks.

Lindsey re-read that email about twenty times before she got up from her desk chair. Her first inclination was to text Rick, but she hesitated. She'd been giving him space just like Athena had recommended, but she didn't want to ruin that or to come off as desperate. But giving someone space always had exceptions for extenuating circumstances, right? And *Shawn Boston* emailing her was extenuating as fuck! So, she shot Rick a quick text.

"I know you don't want to talk to me. But it's important. Shawn Boston emailed me, and I don't know WTF to do."

She paced around her apartment, took a shower, ate some leftover takeout, and paced around some more. Periodically, she checked her phone, but there was nothing from Rick.

By the time she'd gotten dressed in her quarantine uniform (pajama pants, fuzzy toe socks, flip-flops, and an emo rock T-shirt from her middle school days), Lindsey had pretty much decided to ignore Shawn. He had to be fucking with her, right? After all, she and Rick had spent so much time discussing and dissecting Shawn's manipulative language. If he could win his fans over with his charm so easily, who's to say that wasn't what he was doing here, too?

Sure, he'd complimented Lindsey. He'd expressed his supposed love and respect for artists. He acted like he was extending some huge olive branch. But was that just yet another manipulation tactic to make himself look like the good guy and absolve him of his former sins?

Then, another thought hit her. What if this wasn't really Shawn? Anyone could spoof the email "shawn@shawnbostonofficial.com", right?

So, she shot him a quick reply: "Hi Shawn. Thanks for reaching out. Just because you're famous, I figured I'd need to ask. How do I know for sure it's really you?"

Then, she flung her phone down on her bed, flopping on her back to follow. She thought she'd have more time to think this over, but within a couple minutes, her phone buzzed with a reply. She opened up the email, which had a photo of Shawn.

"Haha, fair enough," the email read. "I should've guessed you'd want proof. Here I am!" Attached was a photo of Shawn, standing in his bathroom, taking a mirror selfie. In his hand he held up a piece of white paper with two simple sentences written in Sharpie: "Hi Lindsey/PunkKitty. It's Shawn."

Shawn actually looked kind of hot. Lindsey felt so guilty the second that thought crossed her mind: she hated that she'd said that out loud to Rick, even if it was a joke at the time. But now, she hated that she could acknowledge he *did* look good here, wearing a simple plain white T-shirt that hugged his torso nicely without being so tight as to show off his muscles. His hair looked good, too, styled nicely with some gel, but not in something ostentatious like a pompadour. His eyes and his smile also seemed genuine, as much as it pained her to admit it.

Ugh! But this could just be part of his good-guy act, right? The act that won him so many fans over so many years. She glanced back at her phone to see if Rick had replied. Nothing.

Lindsey's hungover brain decided she'd need serious, honest to goodness, top notch lobby coffee if she wanted to truly sort this out. So, in her pajamas and flip flops, with a cloth mask over her mouth, she headed toward the elevator.

When she reached the lobby, before she could make her usual beeline for the coffee machine, Francisco appeared in front of her. "Lindsey! You are late on the rent!"

"Not this month, Francisco," she countered.

Francisco stepped toward her, blocking her path to the coffee maker. He folded his arms, making himself a blockade.

"You shouldn't try to block me. I thought we had to stay six feet apart," said Lindsey.

Francisco furled his eyebrows, and unless she was mistaken, he was wearing blush. Lindsey couldn't see what his mouth was doing under his medical-style face mask, but she assumed it was frowning. "Yes, you paid me this month's rent. But you were behind! You still owe me!"

Lindsey had been able to pay this month's rent with her ad revenue money from her YouTube videos. But, of course, with how hard her and Rick's subscribers tended to yo-yo, how much money she'd make each month was a crapshoot.

"I am just waiting to get my next check," she said, not

specifying that her check was going to come from YouTube. She couldn't imagine what Francisco's reaction would be if he learned she'd become a YouTube "influencer," if he even knew what that was.

"Well, you'd better have the rest of the rent to me by this coming Friday, or else you'll be back on thin ice!"

Francisco stormed out of the lobby. As Lindsey approached the coffee maker, she felt her phone buzz in the pocket of her pajama pants. She pulled it out to check the email: "Invoice from PackDaddy."

Shit. She'd forgotten that PackDaddy was charging her by the month, just like Francisco was. Lindsey had hoped she wouldn't need PackDaddy's storage services for so long, but that was before ArtCon got canceled. Now, PackDaddy had locked her into a PPP: PackDaddy Payment Plan.

With the payments she was owing PackDaddy, plus the rent she still owed...

She just hoped those YouTube checks would keep coming her way. And that her PunkKitty website sales would keep increasing. But there was no way to know for sure.

If only she could get a *huge* order of PunkKitty merch.

Or something *like* a huge order. A huge art commission. Which was exactly what Shawn was offering. Shawn had the type of money that could completely obliterate her debt.

Maybe she had to hear him out.

When Lindsey got back up to her apartment, steaming cup of coffee in hand, she sat down at her desk and opened her laptop. She pulled up the email from Shawn and re-read it, including his reply with his photo. His eyes and his smile radiated sincerity, but then again, Shawn was used to being watched online. Obviously, he knew how to make himself look like he cared.

Sighing and taking another big gulp of coffee, Lindsey typed her reply.

To: Shawn Boston
  From: Lindsey Drake

Subject: Re: Re: Re: Hey, Lindsey. It's me. I want to talk. I hope you'll hear me out.

Hi, Shawn. Thank you for providing the photo proof so quickly. I know you're really busy. Honestly, I hadn't expected you to reach out to me. But I do appreciate it and I appreciate your kind words about my art. I would be open to hearing about your new project. What kind of art were you looking for and what type of payment were you thinking?

Lindsey assumed this would be the best approach: just keep it professional. Keep it all about the art, not the drama; something Lindsey herself hadn't been able to do over the past month at all.

Shawn's reply came quickly, within five minutes. For such a busy guy with so many followers and so much music to make, he really was able to reply to his emails fast; Lindsey wondered what was up with that.

To: Lindsey Drake
  From: Shawn Boston

· · ·

Subject: Re: Re: Re: Re: Re: Hey, Lindsey. It's me. I want to talk. I hope you'll hear me out.

Hi Lindsey—that's great to hear! Let's talk this afternoon. I have some time at noon pacific. Here's a link to the zoom call I set up for us: zoom.com/shawnboston12354

Talk more than! - Shawn

That's how Lindsey ended up sitting at her computer at two o'clock that afternoon, just a little jittery from her third cup of lobby coffee (thankfully without any further run-ins with Francisco), nervously awaiting a conversation with Shawn.

She hated the fact that she felt nervous at all. Shawn was a celebrity, but he was still just a person. She couldn't tell if her jittery hands were from her coffee, her nervousness to say the right things to Shawn, or from some deep-seated guilt. Shawn had her all kinds of confused. Here he was, offering her tons of money for her art. Yet he was still denying that he'd stolen Athena's art. He had caused her to feel guilty for exposing him, but didn't he deserve it? Was this just more of Shawn's manipulative behavior, or had she really misjudged him this whole time?

Finally, Shawn's face appeared on the Zoom call.

"Hey, Lindsey! Can you hear me, okay?"

Shawn was wearing the same plain white form-fitting T-shirt as he was in the photo, he'd emailed her. His hair looked neat and combed. He looked... pretty normal, actually.

"Yeah, I can hear you. Can you hear me?"

"Yep, all good! Thanks for taking my call!"

"You're welcome. Thanks for reaching out."

Shawn smiled. "Of course. Here's the thing no one tells you about getting big on the internet. Misunderstandings happen all the time. It's easy to just make videos talking *at* each other about it. But I thought it would be better if we talked *to* each other instead. Plus, I really like your art, so it would suck if we had to go on having this manufactured rivalry when in reality, we could be working together."

Lindsey nodded. She kept telling herself to stay skeptical of everything Shawn said, but the truth was, he was just being *nice*. And it was *weird*.

"I agree," she said, nodding.

"So, first of all, since I know you're a hardworking artist and I don't want to waste your time: I'm willing to offer you ten grand."

Lindsey almost choked on her own saliva. She was glad she was sitting at her desk at the laptop instead of holding her phone, because she certainly would've dropped it otherwise. Ten grand. That would cover more than all the rent she owed Francisco, plus the rent for the rest of the year. That would cover the rest of her yearly invoices at PackDaddy. That would make up for the money she'd wasted on ArtCon. That would basically solve all her problems.

"That would be fantastic," she said, trying to keep her voice composed and professional, when internally she was screaming. "I would love to know more about the details of the project."

"Excellent!" Shawn said with a smile. Then, Shawn launched into a detailed description of what he wanted. Lindsey tried to take notes on the notepad next to her, but she kept getting distracted. Shawn talked for a long time; something about her cat design with Shawn's signature pompadour on it? Something about the kitty dressed up in overalls to mirror one of Shawn's pictures from his child-hood in rural Indiana. Something about making a Punk Kitty version of Shawn. She scrawled as much as she could on the notepad as he talked.

"Okay," she said. "I can definitely do this. When do you need it by?"

"Would a month work?"

"Absolutely. I can start working on some rough images and then send you my draft next week, and then you can let me know if you want any changes. We can go through a couple revision phases."

"That sounds great!" Shawn smiled again. It was weird... he seemed genuinely happy to be working with her on this. Lindsey still couldn't tell if she should be relieved or suspicious.

"There was one other thing I wanted to talk about, too," Shawn continued.

The wave of nervousness overtook Lindsey once again. Alarm bells blared in her brain; she'd have to go back on alert. Remember to stay skeptical of everything he says, she told herself. But another part of her brain countered that: *This guy just offered you ten grand, solved all your money problems, and wants to support your art. You can't possibly still hate him. This is getting ridiculous, Lindsey.*

"Sure, what's up?" she asked, trying to keep her voice even.

Shawn sighed. "I really hate that you and your friend feel like I stole her art. Nobody's even told me what her name is."

"She likes to stay private online," Lindsey said. "I mean, after all the drama you and I have had, I can see why. She prefers to just sell in person. It's been rough during the pandemic."

Shawn nodded. "I totally get that. But I really want to

prove to you that I didn't steal it. I'd love for us to be able to publicly squash this beef. But I would never ask you to lie about something. And I truly think it's noble that you wanted to defend your friend's art."

Lindsey nodded. "I mean, I can show you who she is if you want, but you have to keep it to yourself."

"That would be wonderful," Shawn said. "Lindsey, I can't tell you how much it means to me that you're trusting me on this."

Lindsey swallowed, her fingers still tingling with unease. If she shared Athena's name with Shawn, there would be no going back. But she wanted to catch him in his lie. *Or was it possible he was telling the truth?*

"Her name is Athena Angelakos," Lindsey said. "She paints nude portraits of women with fruit."

Shawn's eyebrows wrinkled. "Athena Angelakos, the nude artist? She has an online presence already."

"What?" Lindsey asked.

"Well, I don't know for sure. Like you said, that's not the name it's under. But just going by the fact that her first name is from Greek mythology, and her last name has "angel" in it, and you said she paints nudes... is she the porn artist 'the Goddess Angel' on Tumblr?"

No way. There was no way Athena had a Tumblr. Much less a *porn* Tumblr. And there was no way it was well known enough that *Shawn Boston* was beating off to it...

Lindsey swallowed again, trying to keep her voice calm. "Let me look it up."

Lindsey opened a new tab on her laptop, her fingers flying across the keyboard as she searched for "the Goddess Angel." Sure enough, a blog came up; a page filled with graphic, explicit, hardcore porn. The art style was unmistakable. Though there were no Renaissance-style women and no fruit, that was clearly Athena's art. But it wasn't classy nudity like her convention paintings. These pictures featured men with massive dicks pounding women in the asshole.

Maybe that was why Athena stuck a sharpie in her butt. For reference. Lindsey swallowed the bile building in her throat and tried to wipe that thought from existence.

She clicked to the blog's "about" page.

"Hi. I'm the Goddess Angel. I draw heavenly porn for all of your needs. I don't list my contact information because I don't want anyone who knows me to find this blog, and I like to keep it completely separate from my other art identity. Commissions for full pictures are $100 apiece."

Damn. So that's how Athena was making money—on a porn blog! *And* it made sense that she refused to have any kind of online presence; if someone put together that she was the Goddess Angel, her rich, conservative grandma would stop helping her out with rent. *Damn!*

"Shit, I guess you're right," Lindsey said. She felt a cold wave wash over her; not only had she put together that Athena was running a secret porn blog this whole time, but now *Shawn Boston* knew that too. Holy shit.

"Please," Lindsey begged. "Don't tell anyone that Athena is the Goddess Angel. She really needs to keep things private—"

"Don't worry," said Shawn. "Her secret is safe with me."

Lindsey was starting to wish she'd never answered Shawn's email. She could've just continued this drama war with him. She'd eventually earn ten grand through YouTube revenue if she had just ignored his email, right? But now there was no going back.

"Anyway, back to what I was saying about us squashing our beef," said Shawn. "Would you be willing to make a video together? Where we talk about how we worked out our misunderstanding?"

But you still haven't proven that you didn't steal Athena's art! Lindsey's mind screamed internally. But Shawn was offering her ten grand *and* he now had knowledge about Athena that Lindsey couldn't let get out.

At this point, what could she do except whatever Shawn asked?

"Sure," she said. "Let's make it."

Chapter 18

"Now you wanna talk," Genie texted him back, ignoring his first two calls. "Desperate isn't a good color on you dude."

"I'm sorry!" Rick replied and called a third time. Thankfully she finally answered.

"You bailed on me dude, you bailed on me for some busty troll with an ego bigger than her chest and all you cared about was getting more views. It sucked. It really sucked dude."

"I'm sorry, I'm sorry, I'm so sorry," Rick repeated but each apology bounced back like a tennis ball on a brick wall.

"You can keep saying it, but all I hear is 'I'm a dick, I'm a dick, I'm a dick-dick-dick,'" she practically sang the final three words.

"I deserve it. You're right."

"I know I'm right, of course I'm right. After being friends all these years I woulda thought you'd know I'm always right, so what changed besides Tits McGee?"

"Are you okay?"

"No, I've had a really shitty go lately and needed to talk to my best friend, but he was too busy trying to be famous to care."

"What's wrong?"

"You don't get to pretend to be worried now."

Rick's nails dug into his palm. He could feel his heart pounding in his ears and the more he concentrated on Genie the louder it got. Even his pulse was pounding to her tune. "You're a dick, you're a dick, you're dick-dick-dick."

"My mom's sick again. I've been taking care of her the best I can but it's tough to do that when work is laying everyone off."

"That's awful," Rick wanted to say more but Genie continued.

"We're getting enough now, our aid arrived, I don't need sympathy from you right now, I needed your support all last week when you were too busy." Her voice went up an octave at the end. "And my sister thought she got it from her stupid boyfriend cause she thought lockdown didn't apply to her, so we were all freaking out about possibly having it."

"Did you?"

"No thankfully it was just allergies. I wish I could've seen her get the test, she said she cried."

Rick remained silent. He didn't want to be told to shut up again, so treating their conversation like a busy intersection, he waited for the light to turn green.

"Been keeping up with your videos though. Dick." She laughed this time. Maybe some progress had been made. "Not bad, you two put Shawn in his place."

"You'll never believe what happened," he said and when she didn't cut him off, he recounted the story of the cashier at Rite Aid.

"That dude is definitely stealing organs, though."

"I didn't say I offended him, I said he liked me. If anything, he will steal them for us," Rick laughed.

"Never a bad idea to have an organ thief in your back pocket. Just make sure you never spend any holidays with him."

They continued laughing, having an entire conversation through different volumes and tones of laughter. A short, wheezing cadence kicked back to life by a long drum roll of chuckles. They were making music together once again.

"So, how're things with you and Lindsey?" Genie asked.

Rick bit his cheek. "Well, I don't know. We got in a fight and kinda stopped talking for a couple days. She's sent me a few messages, but I don't know how to respond."

"Wait, the hot girl is sending you messages and you're just ignoring them? Rick, you're a bigger idiot than I thought, and that's saying a lot."

He filled her in on the argument, and how he ghosted her after. Genie laughed in that smug-ass way of hers. "I'm just glad I was apparently right about her. She wants attention and doesn't care how she gets it."

"You don't even know her."

"Of course, I know her, the world knows her—at least the part of her she wants the world to see—and what I've seen is a power-hungry personality with a brain bigger than her chest."

"Well, she's out of my life now, so I guess you can rub it in my face if you want."

"I just did," Genie chuckled then added, "but I think you should be careful. She's not a silent person, so if she's been quiet there's a chance, she's planning something."

"I doubt it," Rick replied and took Genie downstairs. They spoke in his soundproof closet. Thankfully Sven wasn't around, which meant he and his grandpa had gone somewhere private, and Rick played some of Genie's requests.

He tried reaching out to Lindsey the next day but got no response. Maybe it really was over. Scrolling through Shawn's socials, he saw new posts about his album and the pinned apology video throwing Rick under the bus. If it were really over, at least he could put this beef to rest. He could see now that Lindsey wasn't completely wrong in growing a channel off the back of controversy, but how much bigger did he need his channel to get? People started to comment more on his drum videos, and maybe he had enough fans to focus solely on that. He tried typing out several messages to Lindsey, but immediately deleted them. Part of him wasn't sure if he was ready to forgive her, but the other part was supremely horny.

By the end of the week, he had uploaded two more drumming videos, including one Genie begged him for. Rick was on his way upstairs after another drumming session when he bumped into Sven.

"Rick! How've you been? I'm so happy to see you back on the drums again, I was beginning to get worried about you."

"Yeah, things have just been a little crazy lately."

"I know what you mean, my brother was just discharged from the hospital."

"What?"

Sven nodded and a pit grew in Rick's stomach. He was so wrapped up in his own life he had forgotten about a global pandemic. How thick could he get? Thicker than

Lindsey's ass? a girl not talking to him as he drummed safely in the basement of his apartment complex, he hadn't stopped to think about the thousands of people dying every week.

"He'll be okay. His oxygen is back up, but it was really tough for the family these past two weeks."

"Two weeks?" The pit ignited and he nearly choked. Its flames licked his esophagus and he needed water. "I had no idea—" he stopped to cough, covering his mouth with his shirt, and Sven backed away. "I had no idea. I'm so sorry."

"I don't like to talk about things unless it can bring good news, ya know? We feed off each other's energy, and that's one of the reasons I'm so grateful to have Phil in my life. He has been such a positive light, bringing me back to reality whenever my mind wanders too far."

Rick cringed and gave a thumbs up, not sure what else to do. He didn't need to know how great his grandpa was at distracting his romantic partner. The stairwell felt like it shrank to the size of an amp, bouncing their conversation through the halls of the building while pushing their bodies closer together.

"And he really cares about you," Sven added.

"Yeah, yeah, I know." He slipped by Sven and ascended to the top step.

"And he's proud of you."

It was a sentence too far. Rick jogged upstairs. He was panting by the time he reached his apartment, where his grandpa sat in front of the tv eating a bowl of cereal. "Find a job yet?" he asked.

Rick stopped in his tracks. Could he be serious? He showed him how much he made online. Was it even about the money, or was it about the businessman uniform? He had made more money on his drumming videos alone this month than he had from his business degree since graduating. Even Low Octave hired him before he graduated.

"Who do you think is hiring right now?" Rick rounded on him. "Besides I thought the rent was covered."

"Not having to pay rent and having it covered are two completely different things buddy." He wagged his spoon in Rick's face. His feet went up in the recliner and he adjusted his posture. "Someone's still getting paid."

"How much have you brought in this month?" Rick's nostrils flared.

"I still have a *job*." The emphasis his grandpa placed on that last word told Rick exactly what this was all about.

"You barely contract anymore; Dan only calls you in when he's desperate. He told you to retire already and get your social security." His grandfather maximized his payments the previous year and still hadn't started taking out.

"I still got more work in me, that's the difference between you and me. When this is over, I'm back to work, you're just trying to what? Sit in front of a computer all day or play drums?"

"Both have brought in more money this month than you."

"Watch yourself."

Rick didn't have to look at his grandpa to feel his gaze narrow. If looks could spark a flame, the old man was lofting molotovs at gas stations.

"You say you care about me, that you're looking after me for my parents, but you don't. You're just an old fuck who's alone and find pleasure in making me feel like shit. Why is that? Do you want to control my life, so I never leave? Is that it? My dad's gone, grandma's gone, who do you have left? Your loser of a grandson and Sven? Yeah, you're clearly winning at life."

He rose and within seconds was inches from Rick. He could smell milk on his breath. "I'm not the one keeping you around here. You're the one who's been afraid of his own shadow for five years. You want to complain about someone being unfair? Well guess what? Life isn't fair. You're mad at me cause you got a degree? I wanted what was best for you."

"You wanted to control me," Rick shot back. He straightened his spine so his grandpa could no longer hunch over him, but didn't advance. He needed to stand his ground, not conquer more. The wrinkles around his grandpa's eyes deepened. He looked like he was about to take another step forward and bump his chest into Rick, but his muscles deflated. He slumped back down onto the chair and ran his hand over his thinning gray hair.

"Just go." He slid back in the seat and reached for his bowl, hesitated, and pulled his hands back empty.

"Grandpa?"

Phil didn't respond; Rick remained frozen in place. He wasn't sorry. It was his grandpa's fault he was stuck chasing jobs he didn't want, right? Or was it? He was so sure his grandpa set him down his path and any straying would result in an encore performance of their first video, but now—with his grandpa silently sitting four feet away—Rick felt the light burden of his nearly debt-free life. Was it his fault all along? It wasn't his grandpa's money that paid for school—not all of it at least. His grandpa helped with textbooks, but most of the money his parents left them was meant for tuition—"*Specifically, so you can get a job and don't have to rely on anyone,*" his grandpa added when they looked at schools together.

But maybe he was right. He didn't *have* to listen to him, he chose to because the consequences felt too heavy to lift on his own. He had already lost both his parents and, basically, his grandma; losing his grandpa on top of that—even if it cost him his pride—was one relationship too many. Since his grandma left, he hadn't even kept up with her. He saw her posts on social media, but they never texted or called each other. She was too busy taking selfies on dunes and hitting the open road where technology barely rode shotgun. He backed away without saying another word. His jaw clenched too tightly to open anyway. When he reached his room, he felt like he walked into a sandstorm. His eyes watered as he choked on the particles galloping down his throat.

When he finally felt his phone buzz, he was ready to pull a grandma and leave it behind as he hit the highway, however the words "check your messages!!!!!" from Genie broke that daydream and all his limbs went numb when he saw the notification.

YouTube blew up. At least a dozen videos were on his homepage with his face in the thumbnail, the biggest being Lindsey and Shawn's collaboration, followed by a video by the DrawmaLlamas titled "Rick was a Dick the whole time."

This couldn't be happening. He tried to load up YouTube on the computer, but it shut down at his first request. He pulled the app back up on his phone and started watching the videos, one after the other.

There Lindsey was in a low cut shirt, her chest acting as an amplifier capturing all the attention on the platform. The views were skyrocketing. Over 80k and it hadn't even been up for an hour. It was going to be bigger than the first upload of his fight with his grandpa.

Everything she said was either a lie or taken out of context, and it all made Shawn look good. Every time Shawn shared his screen on the stream, Rick noticed the browser windows he had pulled up. One of them intrigued Rick: a Tumblr page called "The Goddess Angel."

Toward the end of the stream, Shawn asked Lindsey, "So, are we cool now? You understand that I didn't steal any art and it was a misunderstanding."

And Lindsey had the audacity to agree with him! "Yeah, I must've been too quick to accuse you, and I apologize."

Shawn's gross, smug-ass face had the balls to *smile* at her. "See? It's not so hard to take accountability on the internet. I just wish Rick would've been willing to come on the stream too."

"I haven't heard from Rick for a while now."

"Maybe he's just trying to hide from everything. I appreciate you having the courage to face this one on one. I wish I could say the same for Rick."

"Yeah, I wish I could too, actually."

Shawn asked another question: "Do you think Rick's just trying to hide from his problems?"

Lindsey sighed. "It sure seems that way."

Rick felt nauseous.

Before calling Genie, he clicked on the next video. As a digital pen outlined a cartoon, a voiceover recounted the Shawn and Lindsey collaboration. "And Big Rick Energy, the smallest dick name I've ever heard of by the way, took it upon himself to continue lying about Shawn's theft for what? Jealousy? You don't ruin someone's life over jealousy, that's some petty-ass bullshit. And all I have to say to you, Rick, is that if you delete your channel, nothing of value will be lost." He couldn't finish the video. How could they milk a 30 minute video out of what Lindsey and Shawn had done? How many synonyms for asshole could they come up with?

He closed the app and messaged Genie back. "Can I

move in with you?"

Before she responded, an unknown number popped up on his screen. His pulse quickened. They couldn't have found him already. Was he doxxed? How many more messages were coming his way?

However, when he opened the text, his eyebrows nearly jumped off his face. "What the fuck did she just do?"

Followed by a second text, "it's Athena by the way."

Athena? Like the Athena who started this whole thing? They had spoken before but always through Lindsey. How did she even get his number?

"Did Shawn not steal from you?"

"Of course, he did, but Lindsey got an offer to work with him if she recanted her story. I'm FURIOUS!!!! And Shawn, how could he! Even after he called for artists to work together. He's so sneaky."

He knew it was bad, but he couldn't believe Athena was this angry. *He* was the one who took the brunt of the attack.

"Did you not see the web page Shawn shared?"

Rick remembered the blog but didn't think much of it. "Yeah, for a second."

"A second? He kept my page up for like, thirty seconds!"

He checked the video again and typed in the site that flashed across the screen. Naked drawings in different sexual encounters were all over the site. The comments were filled with people supporting Shawn and calling out her "disgusting" behavior.

"How could she do this to me?" Athena messaged back as Rick left the site.

"Did she talk to you about it?"

"Not before, but she won't leave me alone now, trying to ask me to understand."

. . .

Rick nodded as he read her messages, but he didn't have much to say. Athena filled him in on all of Lindsey's attempts to reconnect. She started by trying to walk right into Athena's apartment, drunkenly banging on her door at 2 a.m. like an abusive stalker, which Athena said was one of the main reasons she had started to look for new apartments.

"I just can't live in the same building as someone who disrespects me like this. Does she not understand how close she's come to ruining my life?"

Rick could sense the urgency in her messages as she continued to walk him through the regular phone calls and texts from Lindsey. "Then she started blowing up my inboxes on every social media, my email, even the blog she exposed in her video. The nerve," Athena scoffed.

Rick scratched the top of his head as Athena started a video chat with him. "I don't know what to do," he muttered.

"It's obvious, isn't it?" Athena asked.

Rick shook his head Athena continued, "We have to expose her back."

"What!" Rick couldn't believe what he heard. Had they not *just* faced the brunt of a Shawn Boston exposé video? He felt lucky to still find some privacy when he closed his eyes alone in his bedroom. Why would they willfully walk into something like that again? "You can't be serious," Rick said.

"Of course, I am." Athena put her phone down and tied her hair back. What little make up she had on was smeared around her eyes and her nose was red. She hiccupped and continued, "She hurt us, and now she has to pay."

Chapter 19

L indsey thought having $10,000 would feel a lot better than it did.

She awoke on a Thursday morning to a text from Shawn Boston—yeah, they were on *texting* terms now, and it was weird. Especially since she and Rick hadn't texted in weeks.

"Check ur mailbox ;)," Shawn's text read, winky-face emoji and all. Actually, it wasn't even an emoji. It was just a semicolon and a closed parentheses. Just part of Shawn's old-school cool style, Lindsey figured. Full on emojis would be too Zoomer for him.

Lindsey strapped her face mask on and headed down the elevator to the lobby, silently praying that she wouldn't encounter Francisco on the way there.

When she reached the mailroom, she headed to the rows of tiny gray steel mailboxes lined along the wall. She pulled her key ring out of her back pocket and slid the mailbox key in. Once the door swung open, she saw the gold-ticket item sitting in front of her, the item that was supposed to solve all her problems: a flat white envelope.

Lindsey's address typed on the front, a return address in the upper left corner reading "Shawn Boston Enterprises."

She carefully tore open the top of the envelope, not wanting to rip its contents. Once the envelope was open, she slid out a single check, wrapped in a handwritten note.

Lindsey,

Thanks so much for being so open minded. I'm glad we got to work together, and I truly hope we can work together more in the future.

Love,

Shawn Boston

Inside the note was her check. $10,000. The memo line, in Shawn's unmistakable handwriting—the same exact lettering she'd seen on his Sharpie sign in his original email, the same lettering on his handwritten note she'd just read—he'd written, "For art. For Lindsey."

She smiled at it. Having her name so closely associated with her art again felt nice, even if that deep, twisting feeling in her gut still told her she was a sell-out.

Lindsey spent the rest of the morning depositing her new check at the bank, writing checks to give Francisco for the next few months' rent, and paying off her invoice from PackDaddy.

With her rent checks in hand, she headed back through the apartment's lobby and toward Francisco's office. Like always, she felt a little nervous about having to talk to him again, but hopefully this time she'd leave on good terms. After all, Francisco was just trying to pay his own mortgage bills and property taxes, and Lindsey hadn't been the easiest tenant to get along with. Until now.

She swallowed and began her stride toward Francisco's back office.

"I hope you're happy with yourself."

The voice came from somewhere near the coffee maker. Lindsey turned her head to see Athena, her dark hair pulled into a messy bun, wearing an oversized flannel shirt as a dress, leaning against the counter while coffee poured into her cup.

"Athena, I'm glad I ran into you. I was hoping we could—"

"The time has long passed for talking, Lindsey," Athena interrupted. "I hope Shawn paid you well."

"I need to pay my rent, Athena. We don't all have a rich grandma—"

Athena rolled her eyes. "Yeah, you don't. But you do have parents who would probably let you live with them. Yeah, it would suck. I've met your parents. They're annoying as shit. But don't pretend you had no options. You had options and you chose to sell out."

Lindsey swallowed. All she could do was stare at Athena because, to an extent, what she was saying was true.

"I'm just glad you're finally admitting it was about money the whole time," Athena continued, turning back to her coffee cup. "You used to have this whole stupid martyr act where you pretended that you were doing this for me. Like you were *such* a good friend that you were willing to put yourself in the line of fire just to defend me after I got my art stolen. I'm glad that you're finally admitting what we both knew all along: my art getting stolen was just the 'in' you needed to capitalize on the internet drama community."

Lindsey sighed. "That's not entirely true."

"Oh, it's not?" Athena's voice dripped with disdain.

"Then how come when the man who *stole my art* reached out to you offering a fat paycheck, you took him up on his offer with seemingly *zero* hesitation? Why did I see you and Shawn quote-unquote 'squashing your beef' together on a livestream? Where was *I* in all of this?"

"You specifically said you didn't want to be involved! You're the one who told me over and over again that you don't want to have an internet presence—which, by the way—"

"By the way *what*, Lindsey?" Athena's eyes narrowed. "Tread very carefully if you're going where I think you're going with this."

"You have an online presence, Athena. Goddess Angel, Athena Angelakos. You were the one keeping a huge secret from me for years—"

"Yeah, well it's not much of a secret anymore, is it?"

"What do you mean?"

"On your livestream! Shawn had my porn blog pulled up on one of the tabs!"

"He *what?*"

Athena, once again, rolled her eyes; Lindsey wondered if her head ever hurt from all the intense eye rolling, she did. "You were too enamored with the fame Shawn was bringing you to notice. But during the stream, when Shawn was screen sharing and he clicked from one tab to the next, my porn blog—yes, the Goddess Angel, like you said—was visible. He even had it saved as 'Supposedly stole her art' on his bookmark bar. I've already had my Tumblr DMs blowing up with people asking if I'm the girl whose art Shawn stole. My identity is going to be exposed!"

"Oh my God, Athena, I didn't even notice..."

"Yeah. Because you weren't looking. Because none of this was about protecting me in the first place. Let's just hope Grandma never figures out I'm the Goddess Angel, or else I can kiss Rich Grandma Privilege goodbye."

Athena grabbed her now-full cup of coffee off the machine and stormed toward the elevator, ignoring Lindsey's pleas to wait.

Once Athena had disappeared into the elevator, Lindsey headed back toward Francisco's office. Everything sucked: her sort-of online boyfriend wanted nothing to do with her, her best friend was mad at her, and she was a complete sell-out. But at least she had money to pay rent: so, paying rent was what she'd do.

After depositing three rent checks on Francisco's desk, earning a rare smile from him and a surprised look in his eyes (and what could've been blush on his cheeks), Lindsey headed back to her apartment to figure everything out.

The second she sat down on her couch; her phone began buzzing with texts from—of all people—Mom.

Mom: Tony says you're an e-thot!! I don't even know what that means, but Tony says you've become one, and that doesn't sound good! Lindsey call me immediately!

Lindsey tossed her phone aside. She was not going to call her mom. But the buzzing didn't stop.

Mom: I am trying to be accommodating of the fact that you like to sleep until 2 in the afternoon every day like some kind of hoodlum! So, I haven't woken you up with a million calls yet. But I need you to call me ASAP otherwise I am going to blow an entire gasket, Lindsey!!

. . .

Mom: LINDSEY!! Are you getting these messages?! Are you still asleep?!

Mom: Tony says you showed your BOOBS ON THE INTERNET!!! Is that true?! LINDSEY ANSWER ME!!

Mom: Who is Shawn Boston???!!! And why did you show him your BOOBS ON THE INTERNET?!

Mom: Tony says Shawn Boston is a musician. He listens to his albums with Chad. Why are you showing rock stars your BOOBS ON THE INTERNET?!

Lindsey groaned, deciding to send a quick text back.

Lindsey: I am awake. I did not show anyone my boobs on the internet. Why are you still in contact with Chad? Never mind. Don't answer. Just let me be alone today.

But Lindsey's mom wasn't going to let things go that easily. Lindsey should've known saying "I am awake" was going to be an open invitation for her mom to start calling. Lindsey let the first call go to voicemail. But then the second call came. Lindsey's phone had been ringing loudly for 15 straight minutes before she finally answered.

"What is it, Mom?"

"Why did you show a rock star your boobs on the internet?"

"I already told you. I didn't. I have no idea where you got that idea from."

"Tony showed me the video!"

"The video I made with Shawn Boston? I didn't show my boobs in that."

"Oh my God, Lindsey. You know what I mean! You had that skintight low cut tank top on and your whole boobs were basically showing! Out there on the internet for the whole world to see!"

"Mom. I did not show my boobs. I just have a very large chest. Please stop body shaming me."

"What is body shaming? Is that one of your millennial words?"

Lindsey groaned. This was going worse than she thought. "Mom, how about you answer something for me. Why are you still talking to Chad? You know, the guy who cheated on me with, like, fifty people?"

"Oh, because he and Tony are dating now."

Lindsey almost dropped her phone. "My brother is dating my cheating ex. Is that what you just told me?"

"Aw, Lindsey, don't say it like that. I'm happy that Tony finally found someone that makes him happy."

"I didn't even think Tony was gay. Or Chad for that matter..."

"Tony and Chad are both *pansexual*. That's what he told me the other day. That was another new millennial word I had to learn!"

"I don't care if they are pansexual or potsexual or skilletsexual. I am just mad that my brother is now dating the man who cheated on me and probably gave me crabs that one time, and you're just happy for him!"

"Lindsey, if I can, let me give you some motherly advice."

Lindsey slouched down further on the couch and swallowed, bracing herself for whatever crazy shit her mom was about to spew. "Okay."

"Chad is a nice guy. I think he probably felt that you were emotionally and sexually unavailable. I can understand. You're out showing your boobs on the internet all day, but you never made time for Chad. He needed some love. And from what he's said, he felt like you were willing to show your body for everyone but him and it made him feel unloved."

"That was a thousand times worse than anything I could've imagined," Lindsey groaned. "Mom, are you victim blaming me for being cheated on? And claiming that I owed Chad sex just because of *what I was wearing*? Mom, are you fucking serious?"

"Is 'victim blaming' a millennial word too? I will have to look that up."

"Okay I'm going to go now." Lindsey hung up.

Then, she sent a text to Tony: "You're fucking Chad the Cheater? Wow, you're such a great brother. I hope he cheats on you with 50 Starbucks baristas and gives you crabs, too."

She sat up, gripped her phone tightly in her right hand, wound up her arm like she was about to throw the first pitch at a Cubs game, and violently hurled her phone at the wall across from her. She watched her phone sail past the refrigerator and the kitchen sink before it finally smashed into the back wall of her studio unit.

With no phone to distract her, she grabbed a cheap bottle of white wine off the coffee table, brought it to her mouth, and collapsed back onto the couch, guzzling it like a waterfall. When she'd drained over half the bottle, she slammed it back on the coffee table and let herself fall asleep; a nap in the middle of the day, just hours after she'd rolled out of bed. Being the lazy bum, her mom always accused her of being. Everyone already thought she was a big slut and a lazy jobless bum anyway, so why not just be one?

When Lindsey woke up two hours later, she went to see where her phone had landed. She found it lying face-down in the kitchen area. She picked it up and inspected it; the screen was a little cracked but the phone itself was still functional. Not that it mattered—she could just keep sucking Shawn Boston's cock to make tons of money and buy as many replacement phones as she wanted, right?

She had about a hundred texts. Some of them were from Tony, actually trying to appear like the nice guy. She deleted those. Some were from her mom, yelling at her for being such a 'hoodlum' and a 'trollop.' She deleted those as well. One was from Rick's friend Genie, telling her to please never contact Rick again, because she'd betrayed his trust, and Rick deserved better than that, and Rick was a sweet guy who was just trying to make it in this cruel world, and how dare Lindsey use her feminine wiles to lure him into the proverbial e-bedroom before breaking his heart by collabing with a man like Shawn?

Lindsey felt tears beginning to prickle hard at the back of her eyes. A strong headache overtook her, a combination of an incoming hangover and her struggle to hold back the impending tears. She sat on the bathroom floor, still a little drunk, with her phone in her hand.

The rest of her texts were from Shawn.

"Hey, I really like working with you. I know it's weird but… can we please make more magic together?"

Chapter 20

The moment he pressed play; the words came pouring out. He had never laid his voice over a track, but had plenty of experience working with sound and mixing music. Athena helped him with the Lindsey verse because his mind kept going blank the second, he had to say anything besides how gorgeous she was and how hurt he was, but the lyrics that picked apart Shawn fell from his mouth as deftly as snow in February. When they finished the song, Rick uploaded it on YouTube but left the video unlisted until it was time to be released.

"I just want us to make sure this is the right idea," Rick said. He looked at Athena's face through the Zoom screen and sipped a beer she swore by; though he had never been a big drinker, he enjoyed the dense taste of the stout.

"Yeah, yeah, yeah, I'm already reaching out to the DrawmaLlamas," Genie said, her face concealed behind the avatar on the others' screens. She had still not revealed herself to Athena.

"Me too! I am sending them the link now," Athena added

"You two are what!" Rick shouted, nearly spilling his drink. "This wasn't part of the plan!"

"We weren't going to just let it sit there," Athena spoke like it was the most obvious decision in the world. "And they're going to jump at the opportunity to release it. It gives them a chance to look unbiased, which is a golden ticket in the commentary community," she added.

"No, we were supposed to wait and see if this was a good idea." Rick downed the last of his beer, not even enjoying the taste—he just wanted to encourage the dull, warm sensation it brought. His fingers tingled. "I thought we were in this together."

"We were, but you keep talking like you get the majority say," Athena said. "I was just as exposed in that video as you were."

Rick wanted to disagree but didn't have the chance as she continued, "And what was the point of recording all of that if we weren't gonna to release it? I already told you, the longer we wait with a guy like Shawn, the harder it is to fight back—he thrives on apathy. He has all of the momentum right now, and if we wait too long people will just ask why you're bringing this up again."

"Last week you didn't even like the internet at all! Now you suddenly have all these opinions on YouTube culture?" Rick questioned accusingly. "Sounds like you're actually just mad that Shawn exposed your porn Tumblr."

Before Athena could protest, Genie interjected. "She's right dude, there was no point in making the videos in the first place if you weren't gonna upload it. And I know you've still got the hots for Lindsey, but she's still an asshole who put both of you through hell just to get a few thousand more subscribers."

Genie was wrong. Last time Rick looked; Lindsey's page had gained far more than just a few thousand subscribers. But he kept this fact to himself. "I just want to be smart about this; I don't want to bring any more negative attention to ourselves. If they can flip this—"

"But they can't!" Athena cut in. "Which is why it's important that we get it out now while people are still making new videos on the topic."

"Well, you still need me to publish it, it's on my channel," Rick said.

"Yes, which is another reason why I had to send the link out, so if you got cold feet, a large channel like the DrawmaLlamas would still find a way to release it."

"That's manipulative as fuck," Rick replied.

"It was necessary, clearly! If you were letting Lindsay blur your judgment this much, I couldn't take any chances," Athena said.

Rick's stomach rumbled with anxiety. Genie added, "Look, you two just became allies, don't split up already. You did good today, but tensions are clearly high, so let's all just take a deep breath."

Rick knew she was right, and knew there was no way he *wasn't* going to publish the video, especially now. But he hated that he didn't even seem to be part of the discussion. It felt like he was taking four steps back and would once again be nothing more than a kid getting thrown to the ground by his grandpa, the world pointing and laughing at him for *another* five years.

"I'm sorry. I'm just so pissed off, especially at Lindsey," Athena said.

"Good, now Rick," Genie said.

"I'm sorry for losing my cool," Rick said.

"Now that you're not acting like idiots anymore, let's be friends again and have another drink."

They scheduled a time to release the video, and joked about what life would be like if Shawn got abducted by aliens, if Lindsay had a flat chest, and if the world knew how big Rick's dick was.

"I think if Rick was born in an ancient civilization, they would think his dick was God and he was its loyal servant," Genie snorted.

"And on that note, I think I'm gonna head to sleep," he grumbled as he ended the call. Though his body felt numb, and his eyelids felt heavy, he couldn't fall asleep. His heartbeat too fast. He saw every strike they threw at Shawn being countered 10 times harder. It felt like he was trying to run in a straight line on a vinyl record.

He didn't remember falling asleep, but he shot straight up at 6 a.m. and stumbled over a pile of his dirty laundry to his computer. YouTube wouldn't load. If this diss track saved his online career, maybe he would buy a new laptop.

He did his best not to stare at the screen when his channel finally loaded, but the more he tried to look away, the slower time went. Their upload schedules were all set, and he couldn't waiver from publishing his video without messing up everyone else's schedule. Athena and Genie had sent out the video link to various creators, who probably had their uploads planned around its release.

Thankfully his grandpa left the apartment, so he had the whole place to himself. He tried his best to watch a movie but couldn't make it five minutes. He couldn't even drum out his anxiety without fumbling his sticks. His mind jumped back to the video.

He paced in his kitchen nibbling whatever food he could find and counting his steps like the second hand on the clock until finally the video was published. The results were instant.

Even the DrawmaLlamas were at the ready, electing to react to it live which drove even more traffic to the video.

Before he knew it, he passed 10,000 views and the number was climbing faster than he'd ever seen before.

The comments, the likes, and of course the dislikes came flooding in. The initial messages were links to Rick's old viral video. He felt justified deleting them since that video had been out for so long and marked them as spam. But the new comments agreed with the diss track. Not only were they all calling Shawn a dick, but they were complimenting Rick's skill. Some links in the comment section even pointed people to his old drumming videos. He didn't expect one of the primary conversations to be about the quality of the song, but he liked every single one of those comments, even pinning one that said, "Better than anything on Shawn's new album."

As commenters began going at it, Athena found herself live on the DrawmaLlamas' channel, sharing her story. It seemed this was another part of the strategy they hadn't fully discussed, but Rick was relieved to have been left in the dark. He wasn't sure if he would've approved because it meant a brighter spotlight, but clearly Athena had learned a thing or two about marketing, since the longer she was on air the more likes and positive replies they saw.

When Rick dared to go over to Shawn's and Lindsey's latest video, he saw a flood of new messages calling them out:

"Shawn is a liar!"

"Lindsey is a gold digging whore!"

Rick's stomach turned.

"Lindsey sold out her friends to suck Shawn's dick lol"

"Shawn's a fraud!"

Chapter 21

This was worse than Twilight. Lindsey was just the right age to remember her friends going nuts over Team Edward and Team Jacob over a decade ago. But now it was much worse, because these were real-life teams, and she was the girl. And there weren't even any vampires.

The internet was swarming with #TeamShawn and #TeamRick. Ever since Rick had dropped his diss track about her, she'd watched her YouTube subscriber count fluctuate faster than her weight during 420 weekend in college.

Rick's channel was gaining attention fast, too. At this point, it didn't matter that Rick and Lindsey both had die-hard haters; they both had way more fans than they did back when everyone liked both of them. Both of their channels were approaching that magical 1 million subscriber mark. Lindsey was almost on the same playing field as the goddamn DrawmaLlamas!

Lindsey noticed the date on her phone; ArtCon was supposed to be this weekend.

If the stupid COVID pandemic hadn't shut down the

entire world and ruined everything, Lindsey and Athena would've been at ArtCon right now, with Elise Shiloh being the only actual con artist in their midst. They would've been sharing a table, selling their art to passersby. They would've been *friends*.

Instead, ArtCon weekend was spent plugged into the internet. Lindsey sat naked at her desk that Saturday morning, her head aching with a hangover; giant noise-canceling headphones covered her ears. She searched #TeamShawn and #TeamRick in the YouTube search bar all morning, watched every drama video she could find, then refreshed the page to find more.

Some of the videos were from shippers who wanted Lindsey to end up with either Shawn or Rick.

By the time Saturday afternoon rolled around, Lindsey still hadn't put any clothes on, and she still hadn't left her chair. Instead, she was balls-deep in new YouTube searches: this time for all the ship names. PunkKitty x BigRick. Rick x Lindsey. Lindsey x Shawn Boston. Shindsey. Lawn. Seriously, the term "lawn" no longer brought up searches for lawn care tutorials; now it brought up Lindsey x Shawn shipping videos. She watched hours of videos where people had cut footage from Lindsey's videos in with footage from Rick and Shawn's videos to make it look like they were confessing their love to each other. A few people even made animatics with custom fan art. One was tagged "NSFW"—someone had actually gone so far as to draw and animate Lindsey sucking Shawn's literal dick. But hey, she was an artist too; she could at least appreciate the work that went into it

Lindsey's mind vacillated between conflicting emotions all day. On the one hand, it felt weird to be the object of this much public scrutiny. But on the other, it turned her on like nothing she'd ever experienced before.

That evening, Lindsey had another Zoom call scheduled with Shawn. They were planning the promotion of his new album; the one he'd paid her $10k for. Once Lindsey had cashed the check, she briefly considered abandoning Shawn, denouncing him, and trying to win Rick back; but then Rick, the big dick, had continued to ignore her texts, and then he dropped that diss track on her. Then the comment wars began. And the truth was, Shawn was the one reaching out to her. He was the one who told her he wanted her career to succeed. As much as Lindsey hated to admit it, she felt like she was starting to lean toward #TeamShawn.

Lindsey got dressed for the video call with Shawn.

"So, beginning of the month is the big launch! Are you excited?" Shawn asked. Lindsey saw what looked like genuine excitement glowing in his eyes. He looked like a kid on Christmas. Maybe Shawn was serious, she thought. Maybe he cared about his music the way she and Athena cared about their art.

"Yeah," said Lindsey. "I'm really happy with how the cover turned out."

"Me too!" Shawn exclaimed, his smile growing. "Your art is so cute! I'm so glad I hired you."

"I'm glad, too," Lindsey replied flatly. A weird part of her brain felt like she actually meant it, though.

Shawn laughed for a second, running his fingers through his puffed-up hair. The laugh was genuine; it was *cute*, Lindsey thought, disgusted with herself. "Have you seen all the videos that came out about us?" He laughed some more. "Team Shawn and Team Rick. It feels like—"

"Twilight!" they both said at the same time, then broke down into laughter together.

"Except I don't end up with any vampire *or* werewolf dick in the end," said Lindsey, laughing as well.

"Hey, you never know, I might be a werewolf in disguise." Shawn shrugged, laughing.

Does that mean I'm getting his dick? She wondered, but chose not to voice that out loud. Instead, she blurted, "Well, you do have all that hair!" and Shawn just laughed even harder along with her.

"Okay, I'm so glad we're working together! You're so fun! Anyway, let's talk about album promotion. I was thinking you and I could do a big livestream together. People would want to see that, right? I mean, we have a *ship name.*"

"Lawn!" Lindsey laughed. "Like something you fertilize."

Shawn kept laughing. "It's pretty funny. I think we could use it to our advantage, though. Team Shawn is way bigger than Team Rick."

"It is?" Lindsey asked, not quite sure why that made her so sad.

"Yeah," Shawn nodded. "I've been running analytics all day. I even had some of my friends run polls on their sock puppet accounts. Team Shawn is way more popular. People like us together. So, we can stream together on the album's launch day. We can even bait people a little if you want. Flirt on camera or something, if you're comfortable with it."

"Well, I, uh—"

"What am I saying? Of course, you're comfortable with it. You're Team Shawn!"

Was Lindsey on Team Shawn? She just wanted to be on Team Lindsey, but that was definitely not an option out of the hundreds of drama and shipping videos she'd watched this morning.

"I am?" she asked, laughing nervously, hoping her laugh came off flirty rather than anxious.

"I mean, Lindsey, I don't think I have to tell you this, but... half of Team Rick doesn't even like you. They just like Rick."

Lindsey nodded. She'd seen tons of shipping videos, but among those, she saw even more videos that were "Team Rick-Does-His-Own-Thing-Because-He's-Too-Good-for-Lindsey-Because-She-and-Shawn-Are-Both-Toxic."

The hard truth was, both she and Rick stood better chances of their channels growing if she chose Team Shawn. And if she didn't, well... what would happen to her reputation online, then?

And if she ended up getting fully canceled, what would happen to her income? It's not like she had ArtCon this weekend...

Lindsey and Shawn talked over video chat for the next two hours. Together, they planned a huge livestream to launch Shawn's upcoming album. They planned all the ways they'd tease and bait the audience. They planned all the ways they'd flirt, and they even practiced some of it on camera.

They also drank wine on camera together.

By the time the sun had set that night, Lindsey was drunk in her desk chair, still on a video call with Shawn.

"Lindsey, can I tell you a secret?" he asked, his voice slurring.

"Sure," Lindsey giggled back.

"Sometimes I get turned on by the negative attention I get online."

"Oh my God!" she squealed.

"I know, it's weird, right?"

"No," Lindsey said, breaking down into laughter, "I am the same way!"

"Wait, really?" Shawn said, laughing as well. "I thought I was the only one!"

"I totally get it! If someone is shit talking you online—"

"—then it means they're thinking about you—"

"—and anyone thinking about me is hot!"

"Oh my God, you're the first person who gets it!"

They continued laughing, both drinking wine out of a bottle.

"Can I tell *you* a secret?" Lindsey said, still laughing.

"Of course. Team Shawn is a bond for life!"

"I had Zoom sex with Rick." The confession flew out of her mouth like a single multisyllabic word. She covered her face with both hands to stifle her drunk laughter.

"Wait," Shawn's eyes grew wide. "The Rick x Lindsey ship is CANON?"

"It is!" Lindsey exclaimed. "But you're right. He hates me now! And his fans hate me! Because I'm toxic, just like they said!"

"No, you're not toxic!" Shawn was drunk as hell, slurring his words, and still smiling. But every word he said seemed genuine. "Look, Lindsey, we all do what we have to online. But here's the thing, okay? We all want to be the hero. When you're the one who starts the drama, you're the hero. But just for the runtime of that first video. Then, once someone comes in to tell their own side of the story, you're no longer the hero. You're just the person who started shit."

Lindsey nodded. "That's deep, Shawn."

"It's really not. I've just been around on the internet long enough to know this. I've gotten hate comments in my day. Sure, maybe you and Rick were the first ones to 'expose' me in the way that you did. But you don't get millions of viewers without at least a couple thousand people who want to see you die. Over time, you'll find out if you're the kind of person who can't handle criticism. If you're not, that's totally fine. Then you leave the internet influencer world and get a real job. Either that, or you realize you *can* handle it. For some of us, it's more than handling it. For some of us, it's a turn on just to get any kind of attention. You know what I mean?"

Lindsey nodded vigorously. "Yes."

"Now it's my turn to tell a secret. My dick has been rock hard since I woke up this morning. And I don't think it's ever going down."

"Don't you think you might need to see a doctor for that?"

Shawn waved his hand, dismissing Lindsey's concerns. "No, not like that. Not like, *literally* continuously. I just mean, I've been so incredibly aroused by all the attention I'm getting. All day. All the attention *we're* getting."

Lindsey felt a few things in that moment. Her head was spinning, but that was probably from the excess of wine. Her heart was also beating faster than normal. She tried to analyze her situation: Was she terrified or aroused? Guilty or just plain drunk? Was she going to have Zoom sex with Shawn? Was that part of her duty as #TeamShawn now? Would that be a good move for her career, knowing that only half of Team Rick even shipped her and Rick, and the other half just wanted her to die because Rick was a strong independent man who didn't need Lindsey's toxic ass?

"Lindsey," Shawn continued. "I really like you. Like, I really like you, okay?"

Lindsey's heart sped up even more. She hadn't realized that was possible. She felt like her face had been submerged in ice water.

"But I have to tell you one more secret. And it's a big one, okay?"

Shawn was drunk off his ass now; there was no doubt about it.

"What is it?" Lindsey asked.

"Part of me hopes that we've gotten to know each other well enough by now that you'll understand. Another part of me hopes that you'll be too drunk to remember this in the morning."

"What is it?" Lindsey repeated.

"I'm gonna tell you, okay? But after I tell you, please just remember that you're on Team Shawn. And that this is a secret. And that we are going to have an awesome livestream together next week?"

"What is it?" Lindsey asked again, this time laughing a little, half out of amusement and half out of nervousness.

"Oh God, this is why Dave is always telling me not to drink so much," Shawn leaned forward and gripped his head in his hand. "I'm going to regret telling you this. But I have to. Because I like you so much and you need to know!"

"Tell me!" said Lindsey.

"Can you promise me something first? Promise me; swear to me that you'll never tell anyone. And that you won't hate me. And that you'll do the livestream with me. And that you're not wearing a wire."

"I promise!" Lindsey said, still drunkenly laughing. "I promise all of those things! Now, tell me your secret before I have to squeeze it out of you!"

"Okay!" said Shawn. Then, he nervously exhaled. "Lindsey…"

"Yes?"

"Elise and I stole your friend Athena's art."

Chapter 22

R ick never thought he'd have to do something like this. But it was war. And he had to fight the woman he loved with the only weapon he had: a diss track.

Chapter 23

L indsey woke up in her desk chair, neck sore from the
weight of her head on her left shoulder. She wasn't
sure when she'd passed out last night after her conversation
with Shawn. All she knew was that she felt sick, and she
wasn't sure if it was from all the wine sloshing around in
her esophagus or from the severity of the situation, she
was in.

As if waking up sitting in her desk chair weren't bad
enough, she also had to be startled awake in the worst way
possible: her phone loudly dinging from a slew of new
texts. Sitting up straight in her chair and rolling her head
around in a circle, trying to pop her neck and ease the
ache, she reached for her phone on her desk. All these texts
could be from Rick, finally wanting to talk. They could be
from Athena or even from Shawn. But when she looked at
her phone, her worst fear was confirmed: the texts were all
from her mom. And a few from her brother Tony, too.

"Lindsey! Sweetie! Are you awake?"

"Lindsey! It's almost noon! Family zoom call in an
hour!"

"Hey linz. Tony here. Dont tell me u 4got about the zoom call 4 moms bday."

Lindsey glanced at the time on her phone: 12:50. So now she had 10 minutes to get herself presentable enough, and hopefully sober sounding enough, to deal with a family Zoom call. But it was her mom's birthday; as annoying as Mom could be, Lindsey at least owed her a birthday call.

After brushing her teeth, a million times to get the stale aftertaste of cheap wine off her tongue, Lindsey threw on one of the few T-shirts she had with a high enough neckline that her boobs weren't on display, along with a pair of old jeans. While the Panic at the Disco shirt from middle school was a little tight on her now, it was a hell of a lot better than having her mom spend the entire Zoom call complaining about Lindsey's abundant cleavage.

She sat back down at her desk, opened her laptop, and entered the family Zoom call. She was greeted by two screens: one with her parents struggling to look at the camera, and another with Tony. And Chad.

"Hey Lindsey!" her mom waved. Mom was wearing a sparkly tiara with the number "16" on it (she was actually turning 61) and a T-shirt that said, "I'm the birthday girl!" in big, almost illegible cursive.

"What the fuck is Chad doing here?"

Lindsey's mom frowned. "Please, honey, no swearing on my birthday call."

"Chad is here because he's a permanent part of my life and this family," Tony stated matter of factly.

Lindsey felt last night's wine getting hot in her stomach. Her head felt dizzy, and she hoped that she wasn't going to vomit all over the camera. But Chad was not a good antidote for hangovers. She swallowed whatever bile was brewing in her gut and sighed. "Happy birthday, Mom," she said.

"Thanks, sweetie! It's a shame we couldn't all get together for dinner this year. But this pandemic is getting scarier every day!"

Lindsey only half-agreed. Yes, the pandemic was getting scarier, but getting to avoid dinner with her family, with *Chad* there, was probably the best thing to come out of this whole mess.

Other than Rick.

Wait, where did that thought come from? Rick hated her. She was Team Shawn now, right? She'd betrayed Rick for clout, and he wanted nothing to do with her. They'd had one passionate night of Zoom sex. Why was she still so hung up on him?

Suddenly, the hangover nausea returned with a vengeance. She remembered what Shawn had told her last night: his big secret. "Elise and I stole your friend Athena's art."

Shawn had been guilty all along.

Lindsey took a deep breath, trying to calm down enough to focus on the family call.

Tony was droning on and on about some new client that his consulting firm had just acquired. Chad was silent, staring lovingly at Tony and nodding along with everything he said, completely enamored.

"So, what are you up to now, Chad?" Lindsey interrupted.

"Lindsey, sweetie, it's rude to interrupt your brother," said Mom.

"Yeah, but Tony's been talking about his consulting work for like ten minutes straight, and I want to hear what Chad's up to. Are you still a busboy at Starbucks who fucks all the ladies who order a soy macchiato?"

"Lindsey!" her mom yelled. "No swearing on my birthday call."

"Sorry, Mom," said Lindsey. "I mean, are you still having sexual relations with every woman who enters the store?"

Chad shook his head. "I'm in a committed relationship now." He even gave Tony's cheek a little kiss for emphasis.

"Never stopped you before," Lindsey muttered into her coffee.

"Chad has changed for the better, Lindsey," Tony said, putting his arm around Chad's shoulders and making Lindsey *want* to vomit. "You could learn a few things from him."

"What's that supposed to mean?"

"It means that you've been causing drama online all year! I subscribed to your YouTube channel because I wanted to be a supportive brother, but you're getting in all this online beef with celebrities. That can't be good for your mental health."

"I didn't realize that in addition to being the golden child, you're also a mental health expert," Lindsey scoffed, rolling her eyes.

"I'm not a mental health expert," said Tony. "But if I were, I'd say that, based on watching your YouTube channel, you're extra bitter that I'm in a happy relationship right now, whereas you ruined your relationship with that Rick guy just to pander to that famous Shawn dude."

"Brilliant assessment, Tony. But you forgot that I'm actually bitter because your 'happy relationship' is with my cheating ex whose side you took when you kicked me out of your apartment!"

"Kids! No fighting on my birthday!" Lindsey's mom shrieked. "We're all family! Tony and Lindsey, I know the two of you don't approve of each other's choices right now. But let's not forget that we're a family at the end of the day."

Lindsey and Tony both sighed. She felt a slight wave of guilt wash over her; even though her mom was annoying, and even though Tony was completely at fault for this, she still didn't want to ruin her mom's birthday.

"Sorry, Mom," Lindsey apologized, trying to sound as sincere as possible.

"Hey, Lindsey," Tony said, his voice calm now. "I understand why you're mad at me. And I get that you don't really trust me right now. But can I still try to give you some advice? Just so I can feel like a good big brother once in a while?"

"What is it, Tony?"

"I watch all your videos. And I know you're probably stressed right now. And you probably feel like you're in a place you can't get out of. But I promise that you can. You have the power to fix this situation. For as much shit as we give each other, I have a lot of respect for you. I've never known you to give up. You're the one that pursued art even when none of us thought you could make a living off of it. You're the one that made a living, then when the quarantine threatened that income, you're the one that found a way to make it big online. You figure a way into and out of everything, and that's awesome."

Lindsey froze. She hadn't heard a compliment like that from Tony in a long time, definitely not since she'd been living with him and Chad, back before their huge falling out. She almost felt like she had the old Tony back. She tried to block out Chad's smug, punchable face sitting next to him, and she just focused on her brother. "Thank you, Tony," she said.

"That's my kids! One big happy family!" said Lindsey's mom, clapping her hands together excitedly. "Now, let's all sing happy birthday to me!"

All the nausea brewing in Lindsey's gut all day finally reached a peak. She vomited all over the webcam.

While Lindsey searched for the "end call" button, she heard her mom mutter, "Aw, on my birthday?" while Chad snickered in the background. She slammed the button and left the call.

After cleaning bits of liquid vomit out of her keyboard, Lindsey crawled into her bed; she needed to get at least a little bit of sleep lying down, not passed out drunk in a desk chair, if she wanted any hope of her neck recovering. She stretched out her legs, cracked her toe joints, and pulled the duvet up to her neck. But sleep didn't come; all that came was a new wave of thoughts.

As much as she hated to admit it, Tony was right. And until their family call, she'd had no idea that Tony thought that highly of her. She'd neglected her relationship with Tony —for good reasons, since she was still furious with Chad— and now she was realizing that that was making things worse. But even worse, she'd neglected her friendship with Athena. She'd betrayed Rick. Even though she and Rick hadn't known each other for that long, she knew there was potential with him. She and Rick were both the type to care about their art above all else, fearless to call out the phonies like Shawn Boston or Elise Shiloh who made jokes of their careers.

Plus, Rick had been honest with her from the beginning. All of their conversations were real. Shawn didn't even admit to his crimes until he'd been nearly blackout drunk. And let's not forget that Shawn was *guilty* of stealing the art in the first place! Shawn was a manipulator, just like Rick's friend Genie had said.

Fuck. Lindsey was #TeamRick all the way.

Now, she had to figure out how to apologize to Rick. He was out here making whole-ass diss tracks on her. If she tried to call or text him, he'd probably just ignore her. He'd blocked her on Facebook messenger, Snapchat, and Instagram. If she wanted to convince Rick that she was truly sorry, she had to do something big.

Lindsey rolled onto her side in bed, feeling her eyes getting heavier, hoping sleep would come soon. But her phone buzzed loudly.

It was a text from Shawn. "Excited for our livestream next week!"

Suddenly, she had an idea.

Chapter 24

Rick had done numbers before. In fact, seeing five digits on the view counter was nothing out of the ordinary for him since he started doing commentary. What surprised him was the like to dislike ratio. Aiming for Shawn in the past was a death sentence. The sort of fire that finds its way to gasoline and burns down whatever digital house a creator had built for themselves.

But the positive comments kept rolling in. Not only were fans of Shawn calling him out for the recent receipts Athena posted, they were going after Lindsay too. Rick rocked back in his chair. His new computer could process entire videos, and he no longer had to rely on his phone or worry about the computer freezing and crashing. He uploaded another jam session from the previous night with no delay and called Genie.

"You watching this?"

The DrawmaLlamas were dissecting his latest upload. "I didn't expect any of this."

"Pretty cool not to be the butt of the joke," Genie said.

Rick wanted to agree. When he and Lindsay started

this journey, the idea of taking down Shawn was second to building an audience. He always saw this as his chance to play music full time. And now he was closer than ever. But the numbers were still directly linked to Shawn; it always went back to him. No matter how hard he tried to run, there would always be a chain leash yanking him back to Shawn's yard.

The DrawmaLlamas sent him a request to hop on their live stream, but Rick didn't reply. He couldn't bring himself to go on there and answer questions about Lindsey.

"I think you should do it," Genie said.

He didn't reply to her at first. He was done being connected to Shawn, and if he went on their channel all he would accomplish was further burning the Shawn Boston brand into his skin.

Genie turned her camera on—she meant business. It was always strange but nice to see her short black hair and thick, plastic framed glasses. He was far more used to the wild-colored hair of her avatar. "Dude, I don't like how miserable you're looking."

"I don't like how miserable I'm feeling."

"Over Shawn?"

"Over all this, I just want it to be over."

"Then don't go on. You've done what you set out to do —don't give them the views. They're the same people who clowned on you when it was profitable."

He leaned further back in his chair until—CRACK— he fell flat on his back. All that money on a new computer, all those views for internet fame, but his room was still falling apart.

"What happened? You, okay?" Genie called from his phone, which rested against his stack of textbooks from that stupid business degree he never used.

He knew his grandpa was with Sven, and the apartment was empty once more. Being alone. Rick could get online now and find thousands of people who claimed to love him, but it didn't make him feel accepted or wanted.

He was as alone now as he was in the dark bar at Low Octave, serving drinks to strangers who barely tipped. The only time he felt any kind of connection was with Lindsey. Even through a webcam their relationship felt more real than anything he ever felt before. He didn't want to go back to his old life, he wanted to build a new one with her, but Shawn took that away—or she had turned on him.

When he closed his eyes, he couldn't help but remember how kind she was during their late, late night video chats, and how kind she would continue to be as she got to know him. "I think I need a break," he said, climbing back to his feet and rubbing the back of his head. He deleted the DrawmaLlama's request and closed his computer.

He walked downstairs with his phone in his pocket to the one thing that always made sense of his life—his drum kit. Everything made more sense when it had a four beat meter to it. His life was measured by how many steps he could fit in between each kick of the bass drum.

He closed his eyes and grabbed his sticks, picking up a beat and letting the sound engulf him. Each slap pumped his body forward like an independent heartbeat, vibrating his thoughts to the same frequency of his world. The more he played, the more in line with the world he felt. The tension from the DrawmaLlamas disappeared, and his thoughts about Shawn Boston were just another drumbeat.

Nothing else existed except the damp air of the basement and the dripping pipes measuring the distance between his neighbors opening and closing their doors. No matter how deep Rick fell into his head, life continued to happen. No matter how far his consciousness fell into the computer, the world went on. The fastest way to stop Shawn was to close the computer not to engage with him.

The orchestra of the apartment crescendo when the slightly ajar door swung open, and his lanky grandfather burst into the room. Rick dropped his drumsticks and looked up to see bags under his grandpa's eyes, and his thin gray hair messed up in all different directions. The wrinkles on his face were deeper than usual and his baggy white shirt made his slight frame appear even skinnier.

"I'm so sorry. I'm so, so, sorry."

Rick didn't know what to say. He sat there waiting for his grandpa to continue, but all he could do was hold out a phone, like it was the last drop of heat from a dying star. "I can't believe I did this to you; I am so sorry." His voice wavered.

Rick stepped forward, seeing a video that dug into his soul for years. His grandpa flipped him on the concrete, with the ease of a trash bag. Only the man in front of him was nothing like the one on the screen. The distance between the video and reality lengthed as he fell into Rick's arms and sobbed. "I can't believe I did this to you. I can't believe how many people have seen this. I am so sorry. You have to forgive me."

Rick held his grandpa back, rubbing the back of his head as he cried into his shoulder. "It's okay, grandpa. It's all in the past."

"It's not okay. It'll never be okay. I hurt you more than anyone should hurt another person. I can't believe that you've had to live with this for all these years." His grip strengthened, crushing Rick's ribs.

"You get used to it." Rick lied, struggling to take a full breath. In reality, if you want to live in a screen you have to adapt and find a way to defang make the attention.

"I love you. You're the only family I have left, and I love you, I'm so sorry I hurt you. I'm so sorry."

Rick held him tighter. He didn't realize how much he needed to hear this until now. It was one thing to turn the momentum of a video in his favor, but it was another to feel—physically and emotionally—the genuine remorse of the person who did it to him in the first place. It was not his grandpa's fault that those kids recorded and uploaded the video. But that day had haunted him all through school. It was the only reputation he ever had, and one he assumed would follow him forever.

He spent the last five years behind a curtain and was finally pulling them back to feel the sun. He hugged his grandfather back tighter, only it wasn't just to accept his apology; now he wanted to hang on to his comfort.

Back in the apartment Phil made them each a cup of coffee. "You know Sven and I aren't just some casual arrangement, right?" Rick didn't say anything. He was embarrassed enough about thinking his grandpa sucked dick for rent.

"He cares about me. He went through something similar. His partner left him for someone else too. It's tough being alone."

Rick agreed. For the longest time, the only person he had in his life was partially responsible for him being so alone, but they were also all each other had.

Chapter 25

Lindsey was nervous. She looked amazing and she felt like shit; but that was the new normal for 2020, wasn't it? Shawn's livestream to celebrate his new album, the one Lindsey designed the art for, was starting in ten minutes. She sat at her laptop, staring into her webcam, waiting for Shawn to admit her to the "waiting room" for the livestream.

Lindsey had actually taken the time to do her makeup this morning. Instead of just thick black eyeliner, like she wore daily since her days as an emo middle schooler, today she actually followed a makeup tutorial from some YouTube channel called "Cookin' Up Looks" to create a pretty brown and orange gradient in her eyeshadow. And she had some dark red lipstick on, sexy as hell. She put on one of her favorite shirts. Sure, it showed a ton of cleavage, but she'd given up on that battle at this point. Her form-fitting black scoop-neck blouse plunged down her chest, and her velvet choker had a long silver charm that trailed down between her breasts.

She looked beautiful, and she was about to truly cancel Shawn Boston.

Lindsey had everything she needed at the ready. In the middle of her computer screen sat the waiting room for her stream with Shawn. To the left was a Word document with an outline of the points she wanted to make to apologize to Rick. And to the right was her secret weapon; the recording of her Zoom call with Shawn. Her receipts.

"Hey, Lindsey!" Shawn said, a huge smile on his face as he appeared in the waiting room. "Going live in five! Live in five! That rhymes!"

"You should make it a song lyric," Lindsey said, half sarcastically, unsure if Shawn would pick up on her newfound passive aggression.

Shawn just laughed. "Maybe I could! Are you ready to launch this new album together?"

A nervous thrumming coursed through her chest. She swallowed and forced a smile. "Yes. I'm ready."

Shawn grinned. "I'm so excited! This album is going to be so great."

"I hope everyone likes it," she said, her voice starting to quiver, a far cry from the confident, passive-aggressive bitch she was a few minutes ago. The closer they got to going live, the more nervous she got. Lindsey wasn't used to feeling this anxious about a human interaction, especially one where she knew she was in the right. The stakes were high, but she knew what she had to do.

"All right! Let's go live and launch this thing!" Shawn said. Then, in the middle of the screen in front of them, a countdown began. 5, 4, 3, 2, 1...

"And we're live!" Shawn shouted. Lindsey looked at the chat popping up next to their livestream. Messages flashed by one after the other, rapidly appearing in the chat. "Wow," Shawn continued. "Looks like we've got almost a million people watching already! That's amazing! You guys are the best! Thanks so much for coming to my album launch."

Lindsey swallowed hard again. A million people were watching right now. She couldn't fuck this up, or else she'd not only lose Rick forever; she'd also lose Shawn (which, considering the circumstances, wasn't that great of a loss) and probably her entire following on YouTube.

"Today, I have a special guest on my stream. Lindsey of Punk Kitty!" Shawn announced. "Lindsey and I have had such a strange journey this year, but I think that's true for everyone. 2020 was so weird. Can I get a thumbs up in the chat for everyone who agrees that 2020 was *so weird*?!"

Lindsey watched as a slew of thumbs-up emojis spilled into the chat. Shawn knew how to drive engagement.

"This year was super weird for me in more ways than one," Shawn continued. "I got canceled earlier this year, by the lovely lady Lindsey next to me. Now, a lot of you might think that Lindsey and I still have some kind of beef, but we don't. Cancel culture is a huge problem online right now. Everyone wants to expose each other. But Lindsey and I are proof that if you take the time to talk to each other and get to know each other on a personal level, most problems can be solved. We hold no animosity toward each other now, and we're excited to announce our collab! Lindsey, can you tell everyone about what we've created?"

Lindsey took a deep breath. She'd have to play along at least for a little bit first. If she jumped on Shawn too quickly with her secret weapon, she wouldn't have time to get in her apology to Rick. She needed to act fast before Shawn shut down the livestream once he knew what she was really up to. But she couldn't reveal that too soon. She had to keep Shawn's trust for a little while. But she knew

Rick and Athena were probably both watching and she couldn't lose their interest either.

"Yes," Lindsey said. "Shawn contacted me to design the art for his new album cover. So, Shawn's new album cover reveal is here, featuring my character Punk Kitty."

Shawn shared his screen and showed off the album. "Lindsey's art is fantastic. I wanted to prove to her, and to all of you, that I truly do support artists and would never steal art. I paid Lindsey for her work."

The chat filled with Lindsey x Shawn memes: *#Team-Shawn. SHINDSEY SHIPPERS UNITE! #LAWN4LYFE!*

"Lindsey, it seems like everyone in the chat likes us together," he laughed. "Can you tell everyone about the process of designing the album art?"

"Yes," said Lindsey. Here we go, she thought. She took a deep breath, knowing that she had to spit everything out rapid fire. "Can you let me share my screen so I can show everyone my art program?" she asked calmly.

"Of course," said Shawn.

Shawn still seemed oblivious, lost in his own world of excitement about his album release. He looked like he hadn't noticed yet that Lindsey wasn't sharing Photoshop, but instead had shared a video—a recording of the two of them drunk as skunks and looking sloppy as hell.

She hit play.

"Can you promise me something first?" Shawn's voice said on the Zoom call recording. "Promise me; swear to me that you'll never tell anyone. And that you won't hate me. And that you'll do the livestream with me. And that you're not wearing a wire."

"I promise!" Lindsey's drunk voice replied. "I promise all of those things! Now, tell me your secret before I have to squeeze it out of you!"

"Okay!" said Shawn. Then, he nervously exhaled. "Lindsey..."

"Yes?"

"Elise and I stole your friend Athena's art."

Lindsey abruptly stopped sharing her screen as she watched the expression on Shawn's face quickly turn to one of shock, his eyes growing wide. Almost as suddenly, his eyebrows furrowed; his face now looked both confused and scared.

Lindsey didn't have time to think about his reaction. She started talking as fast as she possibly could, channeling big Ben Shapiro energy (but with emotional honesty instead of bigotry). "Rick and Athena, I'm so sorry. You two are the greatest people in my life and I ruined it just to work with someone like Shawn. Shawn was really an art thief the whole time, and now you all saw him admit it to me. Rick, I'm so sorry, please forgive me. I understand if you don't want to talk to me anymore; I was awful to you. But if you have any ounce of forgiveness in you, or any willingness to give me a second chance, I'd really like to try again. Athena, I won't talk about you online anymore. You didn't deserve that. You were right, deep down I cared more about my own gain online than your desire for privacy. I'm so sorry—"

LIVESTREAM ENDED.

"What the fuck was that?" Shawn shouted. "I thought you said—"

"I've made my decision. I don't care if it ruins my online career. I'm #TeamRick."

Chapter 26

I f happiness was a person, why would he run away from
it? Rick sat alone in his room with more love on the
internet than he had ever had before. Thousands of people
without profile pictures or names were defending him,
storming the castles of those who wished to take him down
and demanding justice where they perceived wrongdoing.
It was no longer a fight *for* Rick or trying to right a very
specific wrong. It was an imbalanced world, and the opportunity to correct it in a minor action was all that mattered.
Maybe that was why mobs were so popular. The smallest
push forward could catapult an incalculable amount of
momentum and destroy someone's life. And if their life
was destroyed, then certainly those who attacked were
better off. Every person who commented and shared that
original video of Rick's grandfather throwing him to the
ground—they had all been thrown to the ground in their
own way and wanted to know that someone out there hurt
more than them.

Now, rick was being elevated as the other side of the
seesaw fell. He was being raised up high, and he knew it

was only a matter of time before he fell once more, and someone perceived *him* as the injustice that needed to be corrected. No matter what he did this momentum would never last and the best he could hope for was hopping off under his own power.

He was as alone in his room as he was when he started his journey, only now he had accepted his grandpa's apology and could walk to the local pharmacy as a person, not a meme. The problem was always bringing the screen into his life, instead of unplugging once and for all. Now he had two separate lives he could fully live. One brought him money, the other he hoped brought him love. There was still more to do.

His phone buzzed; Genie had messaged him. "You need to go look at YouTube. Now." He ran to his new computer and pulled up the website, where he saw Lindsey was trending.

Forgetting until that point that he had her muted everywhere, he realized she had been sending him multiple paragraphs-long messages apologizing in different ways. The title of her latest video was an apology as well.

He watched it through with Genie, and hoped that, for once, his digital world wasn't lying to him. If views were tithings and apologies were confessions, this could be her attempt to re-enter paradise, but something about it felt sincere. Maybe it was the off camera apologies or the fact she wasn't crying. It was a Lindsey he recognized.

She ended her apology with a call for Rick to reach out. He hesitated, wanting to believe they could put it all behind them. If he could forgive his grandpa so enthusiastically then this should be easy. But his grandpa wasn't behind a camera generating views or income off his apology.

"I wanna believe it's real dude, I really do," Genie said.

Rick's tongue felt numb. He took a sip of water and said, "I do, too. I really do."

"You miss her."

"A lot."

"There's only one way to know for sure then, dude."

"You're always so smart."

"It's why you keep me around," Genie said with her camera on and a wide smile visible. "Call her."

Rick did as she said, and Lindsey answered on the first ring. She smiled as soon as she saw him. "Rick!" she said enthusiastically. Rick wanted to jump through the screen and hold her.

"I saw your video."

"I've missed you so much."

"I've missed you too." He said he was ready to kiss the camera if it meant their lips could touch.

"I've missed you so much," Lindsey sighed. "Everything about you, you were the only real thing in my life worth keeping—and I needed something real to finally go right."

"I just want you. I don't want any of this bullshit. These games have been nothing but trouble for me. I started doing this to make music, but then I barely played when we got involved with Shawn. I was miserable."

"I can't walk away—not yet, but I need you back."

"What do you mean you 'need me'?" Rick asked, unsure what she meant by that now.

"I just need you. Not BigRickEnergy, just you," she replied softly.

"No more videos?"

"You can delete the channel right now if you want."

"Well, maybe there's a way we can work together again. If we leave the drama behind."

They released one more collaboration—a more family-friendly one this time. Rick titled it "Enemies to Lovers", and Lindsey uploaded it to her channel. Though he knew the commentary community would think it was a publicity stunt, all that mattered was that he and Lindsey knew it was real. Rick closed his laptop screen one last time and was about to head downstairs to his kit when he received a picture from Lindsey—one that had him rushing back to his computer. Maybe completely unplugging would be more difficult than he thought, but it was definitely going to be worth it.

Acknowledgments

This book was written for about 30 people we see daily. So as long as they like it, we win. Thank you.

Thank you to Amanda for amandafesting your editing service— you go Glen Coco

Thank you to Keylin's Astre Encre for designing our cover. You're our favorite Degrassi star.

Subscribe to PewDiePie

About the Author

Savy is Chicago's local big tiddy goth GF and YouTube's resident gay aunt from the 80s. Watch her be toxically masculine with her bro RK on Your Morning Guru every day at 9 Eastern, or watch her prove the stereotype that bisexual women love attention on her YouTube channel SAVY WRITES BOOKS.

About the Author

RK Gold exists

Also by Savy Leiser

90s Kids

One Final Vinyl

Sculpt Yourself

SavvyBusinessOwner

Furever Home Friends Series

Also by RK

Lost in the Clouds

Father in the Forest

Beds Are For Flowers

Made in the USA
Columbia, SC
06 January 2022

53667121R00145